Praise for *An Amateur's Guide to the Night*

"The writing is cool and detached, controlling a breathtaking compassion. Her subjects and characters, mostly family members, are right out of life. *An Amateur's Guide to the Night* continues Robison's practice of penetrating the heart. There is not one story in this collection that does not evoke an emotional response . . . It's an intimate, enriching experience."

—*San Francisco Chronicle*

"These thirteen stories are glimpses from a moving train into lit parlors, dinettes, bedrooms and dens. Though the rider sees only fragments, he can intuit essentials from posture, from motion, and see the space that characters inhabit. Think of Robison as the engineer, blowing the whistle, calling the stops and starts; invisible when you want to ask her why we're stalled here in the middle of nowhere, between stations, jobs, relationships and decisions. Like Ann Beattie, Robison shunts the reader off the mainline to a limbo where everyone waits for something to begin or end. As narrative, the stories are inconclusive; as commentaries on the way Americans live now, they're absolute and final."

—*Los Angeles Times*

"It's my hope that *An Amateur's Guide to the Night* will win her the readership she deserves. No American short story writer speaks to our time more urgently or fondly than Robison."

—DAVID LEAVITT, *The Village Voice*

"Hip, deadpan, it's-cute-to-be-crazy stories from the author of *Days* and the novel *Oh!*—with vague grim undercurrents beneath the bright little pop-artish sketches of disaffected youngish people."
                                                                    —*Kirkus Reviews*

An
Amateur's
Guide to
the Night

ALSO BY MARY ROBISON

Believe Them
Days
Oh!
One D.O.A., One on the Way
Subtraction
Tell Me
Why Did I Ever

An Amateur's Guide to the Night

STORIES

MARY ROBISON

COUNTERPOINT

Berkeley, California

An Amateur's Guide to the Night

Copyright © 1981, 1982, 1983 by Mary Robison
First Counterpoint paperback edition: 2019

First published in the United States in 1983 by Alfred A. Knopf, Inc.

All rights reserved under International and Pan-American Copyright Conventions. No part of this book may be used or reproduced in any manner whatsoever without written permission from the publisher, except in the case of brief quotations embodied in critical articles and reviews.

This book is a work of fiction. Names, characters, places, and incidents are the product of the author's imagination or are used fictitiously. Any resemblance to actual events is unintended and entirely coincidental.

Library of Congress Cataloging-in-Publication Data
Names: Robison, Mary, author.
Title: An amateur's guide to the night / by Mary Robison.
Description: First Counterpoint paperback edition. | Berkeley, CA : Counterpoint, 2019.
Identifiers: LCCN 2018033436 | ISBN 9781640090897
Classification: LCC PS3568.O317 A6 2019 | DDC 813/.54—dc23
LC record available at https://lccn.loc.gov/2018033436

Cover design by Jenny Carrow
Book design by Jordan Koluch

COUNTERPOINT
2560 Ninth Street, Suite 318
Berkeley, CA 94710
www.counterpointpress.com

Printed in the United States of America

For My Mom:
Hey, Betty Reiss!

Contents

An Amateur's Guide to the Night

The Dictionary
in the Laundry Chute

ED WAS IN THE BEDROOM, BARBERING HIS HAIR with scissors, when his wife, Angela, wheeled in a vacuum cleaner and moved it around, catching some of the clippings that were clumped on the carpet.

"Aghh, this stuff's all over my neck," Ed said over the noise. "I gotta take a shower."

"I should quit, too," Angela shouted. She straightened up and snapped the toggle switch on the vacuum cleaner. "I need a blouse ironed for tonight."

She wheeled the sweeper into the hall, where she stooped to extract the electric plug from the wall socket. "Come on, you," she said, jerking the cord.

Ed had pulled off his polo shirt. He wadded it and dusted his throat and shoulders. "What's tonight again?" he said. "I forgot."

"Honey, we've talked about it," Angela said from the hall. "Dr. Grosh is coming over as a favor to me. He's going to have a little session with Margaret, and then together we're going to see if we can't get her to eat something. What do you think I should fix, by the way? I mean, for dinner."

"I don't know," Ed said.

"Well, what do you feel like eating?"

"Nothing. I'm not hungry lately," Ed said. "Maybe Sid Grosh should wave his magic wand over me, too, while he's at it."

Angela came and leaned on the doorjamb with her arms crossed. "It's nothing to joke about," she said.

"I'm serious," Ed said. "I think there's something wrong with me. My heart. My pulse bangs in my ears when I climb steps or come up that hill from the fifteenth green. And whenever I close my eyes anymore, I see nothing but bright pink."

"One person at a time," Angela said. "And I'm sorry if this sounds callous, Ed, but right now it's Margaret I have to worry about." Angela went back to the vacuum cleaner and began winding the electric cord around its handle. "Though if anybody can work a miracle with that girl, Dr. Grosh can. He helped us through the time she came back from Lake Point with the whole side of her Rabbit smashed in."

"I wish someone could have helped the car," Ed said.

"He got Margaret calmed down and back on earth and got her sleeping," Angela said.

"Yeah," Ed said. He undid his belt buckle, dropped his trousers, and stepped out of them. "I just pray we're not putting too much pressure on Margaret. This is still her first week out of the whatever-you-call-it."

"Sid Grosh isn't pressure," Angela said.

"Well, good," Ed said, flapping his slacks to shake off the hair.

Angela was backing the sweeper around. She straightened its wheels and aimed it for its parking place, in the back of a utility closet.

"She's got the blues," Ed said, and Angela made a little jump and gasped.

"My God, you startled me!" she said. "I thought you were in the bathroom."

"Don't you think that's it?" Ed said. "What you and I would call the blues?"

ED HAD SEATED HIMSELF AT HIS DAUGHTER'S VANITY table. He had his navy bathrobe on over an untucked white shirt and a pair of dark slacks. His bare feet were filmed with talcum powder. He sat at the vanity table and bobbed his head around, examining his haircut in Margaret's mirror.

His daughter was curled up in the corner, on her bed, with her back against a foam bolster pillow. She was twenty-two, but her face looked puffy and middle-aged. Her hair was dry and wiry, with a zigzag center part. She had one leg drawn up and was embroidering with bright-colored thread on the knee of her jeans.

"Stop whistling," she told her father.

"Him?" Ed pointed at his reflection and said, "Stop whistling" to the mirror. He glanced around to see if Margaret was smiling.

She wasn't, and Ed continued to tip his head. "Why do I have to look like that?" he said.

He got up and went over to Margaret's bed. "What do you think of your new dad?" He showed her his haircut.

"Fine," Margaret said.

"But cheap," he said, "right? For doing it myself."

"No," she said. She relaxed her knee and scooted down on the bed. She got onto her side and stared at the doorknob of her clothes closet.

"Well, your mother says I'm cheap," Ed said. "And maybe I am—about certain things." He plopped onto the bed by Margaret's feet. "But I never cut corners when it comes to you, do I?" He reached over and massaged one of her ankles until she snapped the foot away, saying, "Quit."

"Have I ever? Have I once cut any corners when it came to my daughter?" he said. "Tell me if I have. You can tell me."

"Are you nuts?" Margaret said.

"Okay, okay," Ed said. He started whistling again.

Margaret glared at him.

He kept on whistling. He got off the bed and strolled over to a study desk where there was a small hi-fi set. "What do you know?" Ed said. "My records."

He got down on his hands and knees on the sculptured carpet and hefted twenty-some long-playing albums from under the table. He propped the albums against the wall and began flipping through them, sitting on his feet. "Do you mind?" he said to Margaret's strained face. "A couple of these are records of mine that your mom said she'd pitched out a long time ago. This one's mine." He set aside a Fred Astaire album. "It's got 'A Foggy Day' on it. Did you ever listen to 'A Foggy Day'? I love that song. This one's mine, too."

"Raggedy Ann?" said a man's voice from outside the bedroom door.

"What on earth?" Ed said. He turned on his kneecaps and looked at the door.

"It's Dr. Grosh," Margaret said. She sat up. "He calls me that because I'm Margaret *Anne*. Come on in, Sid."

"Oh," Ed said.

He smiled for Dr. Grosh and stayed standing on his knees to shake hands. "It's good of you to come, Sid. Forgive the bathrobe. I got lost in some old records here with Margaret Anne."

"I'm a little early, as usual," Dr. Grosh said. He laughed deeply and winked at Margaret. He was in his forties but had a kid's face drizzled with dark freckles. His hair was wet, and he wore a black blazer with a pair of muted-plaid pants. There were beads of rainwater on his polished shoes.

"Cats and dogs out there?" Ed said.

"Well, there won't be any flooding in any but the lowest underpasses," Dr. Grosh said. "And we need the April showers. But it slows one down on the road, if one has any sense." He winked again at Margaret, who was nodding seriously as she listened.

"The weather mixed me all up today," Ed said. He clutched the skirt of his robe and got to his feet. "It was so godawful pretty this afternoon, I closed the shop up ahead of time to get in some golf. But before I got halfway home—"

"What's your business, Ed?" Dr. Grosh said.

"Optometry," Ed said. "I'm with Dr. Cravy out at the old mall. Wife says you could tell it a mile away because of my lousy posture. You know, from hunching over the grinder all day— which I don't really do, of course. And then it's funny, too, that no one in the damn family even wears glasses."

Ed smiled and waggled his head at the album he was holding in his left hand.

"Eating?" Dr. Grosh said to Margaret.

"She isn't," Ed said. "That's one of the main reasons why I

think Angela got you over here, Sid. To see if we can get some good hot food down Margaret Anne here."

"I was asking Margaret," Dr. Grosh said quietly.

"Oh, I'm sorry," Ed said. "Lordy, what's my problem? It's time I got out of here."

He moved carefully to the door. He was trying to close it noiselessly behind him when Dr. Grosh said, "Ed?"

"Yes?"

"We may want to have our supper up here in the bedroom, Margaret and I."

Ed opened the door a little. "No sweat," he said. "You just persuade Margaret to eat it. You do that, and I don't care if you build a bonfire up here and roast franks. I mean it." He shut the door.

IN THE HALLWAY, HE STOPPED AND FLIPPED OPEN the laundry chute. He crouched under the small door and called, "Angela!" He tried again, a little louder, and then he got a cigarette from his robe pocket, lit it, and waited, holding up the door.

"What, Ed?" Angela's muffled voice was coming from the chute drop just off the kitchen.

"Can you hear me?" Ed said. "There's a pair of pants or something stuck about halfway down. I'm not quite dressed yet, honey, but you might want to know that Sid thinks he and Margaret ought to eat up here in her bedroom."

"He does?" Angela said disappointedly.

"He didn't say for sure," Ed said, "but that's the way it looks.

Now get your head out of the way for a minute. I'm going to drop the dictionary down to see if I can get the chute clear."

"WILL YOU LOOK AT THIS?" ANGELA SAID TO ED, AND she showed him a plate with some scraps of roast beef and a baked potato.

Ed made a praying gesture and rolled his eyes to the ceiling. "Hallelujah!" he said.

"She ate everything but the fat," Angela said. "Look at *this*." She hurried to the rattan dinner tray she had just brought down from Margaret's bedroom and took Ed an empty mug and a parfait glass. "The coffee and the mousse," Angela said. "Gone!"

"Are you sure Sid didn't eat Margaret's for seconds?" Ed said.

Angela shot him her angriest look.

They were in the kitchen. Ed was finishing his meal at the circular breakfast table.

"He's giving her a sedative later so she can finally get some rest," Angela said.

"Food, sleep," Ed said. "Tomorrow we'll have a new Margaret."

Angela went to the sink and pulled out the dish rinser. She began to spritz the plates from the dinner tray. "He's testing motor mechanisms now, and asking questions," she said. "You're to take him some more coffee when it's perked."

"Right," Ed said.

He loosened his tie knot and unbuttoned his collar. He got up and at the kitchen counter he stood behind Angela with his hands on her shoulders. She moved away and bent over to load plates on the rubber racks of the dishwasher.

"I'm actually *excited*," Angela said.

"It's the light at the end of the tunnel," Ed said, "and *you*. Even you're all lit up."

Angela was wearing a starched blouse with a new straight skirt—at least, new to Ed—and a string of cultured pearls.

"What were they doing when you went upstairs?" Ed said.

"Margaret was following Sid's finger with her eyes, and without moving her head," Angela said. She looked up at Ed and beamed. "We all got to laughing—Margaret, too—about how funny her Rabbit looked last summer after she bashed it up. Like an accordion. We couldn't help it, we just got the giggles."

"Wowie," Ed said.

"I know," Angela said. "Margaret giggling."

Ed brought his dishes to the sink to rinse them.

HE WAS ARRANGING COFFEE CUPS AND SAUCERS ON the rattan tray to take upstairs when he heard Angela say, "Well, look who's coming to see us."

He turned as his wife hurried to Margaret, who was standing in the kitchen doorway with a pink baby blanket around her shoulders. Angela hugged Margaret and kissed her cheek. Margaret was blinking in the kitchen light—her eyes large, her face blank.

Dr. Grosh followed the two women into the room. "We've had a little medication," he said.

"Well, you're just in time for coffee," Ed said. He pulled up the knot in his tie and drew a straight chair from the table for Margaret. Angela eased her daughter into the chair.

"For pity's sake," Margaret said, her words dragging a little. "I'm not dying or anything."

"We know that, baby," Angela said. "We're just delighted. Can't we be delighted in our old age?" She turned to Dr. Grosh. "Sid, how did you manage to pry her from that bed?"

Dr. Grosh moved behind Margaret and then frowned at Angela and shook his head no. Aloud, he said, "I gave her the routine spiel for crazy nuts and then I promised her another crack at your chocolate mousse. That was actually what did it."

"Well, hell, Sid—it's all gone," Ed said.

"Not to worry," Dr. Grosh said. "We can live without it."

"Without it," Margaret said.

"Is she all right?" Ed said.

"She'll be wonderful," Dr. Grosh said. He was still behind Margaret, and he began massaging her shoulders. "Didn't I hear a rumor about coffee?"

Ed was using both hands, hunting in his jacket pockets for his cigarette package.

"Ed?" Angela said, meaning he should serve. She'd drawn up a chair and was sitting, covering one of Margaret's hands with both of her own.

Ed poured coffee and put out milk and sugar. Dr. Grosh had taken the chair on the other side of Margaret, so Ed ended up with a seat facing the three of them.

"It's hot, and I don't want you to have too much," Dr. Grosh told Margaret. He put his arm over her shoulder and held his cup under her nose.

Angela leaned forward and watched Margaret sip coffee. "That's my girl," Angela said.

"Mom . . ." said Margaret.

Ed found his Lucky Strikes in the breast pocket of his shirt. "Jeez, it was a gunky winter," he said, lighting his cigarette. "You know? And this spring hasn't been so good up to now, either. You know, Margaret?"

"Not so good," she said.

"But the thing is, to stick in there and we'll maybe think about school again," Ed said. "Maybe even summer semester. All right, Sid?"

"The thing tonight is sleep, and the thing tomorrow is to eat more," Dr. Grosh said.

"Amen," Angela said.

Ed said, "Oh, of course. Of course, *that*."

"First things first," Dr. Grosh said. "Now. I need to talk to Angela for a minute or so. Margaret, your dad will want to keep you company here. And Ed, it's a little effort for her to talk, so you'll have to do more than just hold up your end of the conversation."

"Right, Sid," Ed said. "We'll be okay—won't we, Margaret?"

"Don't be gone long, though," Margaret said to Dr. Grosh.

ANGELA WAS SNIFFLING INTO HER PILLOW. IT WAS two or three o'clock—Ed couldn't see his watch—and she'd been sobbing off and on since Dr. Grosh and she had put Margaret into bed and made sure she was asleep.

Ed was seated now on the end of the mattress, smoking, even though his mouth and tongue felt scraped and sore from too many cigarettes. "One more time, honey," he said. "Could you try to explain?"

Angela began to speak into the pillow in a small voice.

"Again," Ed said. "I can't hear you."

Angela rolled onto her back. She'd gone to bed fully dressed, and Ed could hear her pearls clicking at her neck. "It's worse than we thought. It's worse than they thought at Saint Stephen's even," she said. "Margaret is hearing voices."

"I know, but what Sid told me . . ." Ed said.

"Our Margaret is sick. That's a very bad sign, hearing voices. It's the worst. And the sad, sad thing is that we were so happy." Angela's voice broke.

"I know, I agree. But what Sid told me is that it's pretty normal, really. I mean it's worrisome, and we've got to watch her, but it's normal that if you don't eat or sleep for a week you can hear things, or even see things."

"Sid's a miracle worker," Angela said.

"Well, what I want to know is did he tell you something he didn't tell me? Something that upset you?" Ed said. "Because I have a right to know. She's my kid, too." Ed felt the heat of his cigarette's tip near his fingernails. He mashed the butt in the ashtray between his feet. "Because what Sid said to me finally was, 'It's normal.' He said after she's slept awhile, the voices will go away."

"He was protecting us," Angela said. "I know what disembodied voices mean. He's planning to go easy on us. That's his way."

Ed crossed to the room's single window and peeped out between the heavy drapes. A fine drizzle was putting a shine on the cars in the condominium parking lot. The light from the post lamps was misted and bleary.

"Whew," Ed said. "Going to be a foggy day in London town."

"What?" Angela said weakly.

"Nothing," Ed said. He turned from the window. "Margaret's okay, honey. So we treat her with kid gloves for a while. We keep her away from the drinking. Make sure she takes those pills Sid wrote up for her. Feed her like a calf for the fair. That's all we got to do. Isn't it?"

"Yes," Angela said.

Ed looked out the window again. He tried not to part the drapes too much. He didn't want to bother Angela with the light. "Well, then I don't get it," Ed said. "Honest, I don't get it. I mean, I don't see why we aren't happier and why we can't *all* get a little sleep around here."

An Amateur's Guide to the Night

STARS WERE SOMETHING, SINCE I'D FOUND OUT which was which. I was smiling at Epsilon Lyrae through the front windshield of my date's Honda Civic—my date, a much older man who, I would've bet, had washed his curly hair with Herbal Essence. Behind us, in the little back seat, my date's friend was kissing my mom.

I could see Epsilon, and two weeks before, when I biked all the way to a veterans' cemetery outside Terre Haute, I had been able to separate Epsilon's quadruple stars—the yellows and the blues—with just my binoculars. I had been way up on the hill there, making a smeary-red glow in the night with my flashlight. The beam had red cellophane taped on it, so I wouldn't desensitize my night vision, which always took an hour to get working well. My star chart and the sky had made sense entirely then, and though it was stinging cold for late spring, I stayed awhile.

It was cold now, or our dates would have walked us away from the car for some privacy.

Mom was with the cuter guy, Kevin. She always got the lookers, even though she was just five feet tall. She wore platform shoes all the time because of it. That was her answer.

My problem was my hair. It was so stick-straight that I had had it cut like the model Esmé—a bad mistake.

I could hear Mom telling her date, "I woke up this morning and the car was gone."

"Sounds like a blues song," he said.

And now she was saying, "It's time for our beddy-bye. Sis has classes tomorrow."

MOM AND I PASSED FOR SISTERS. WE DID IT ALL THE time. I was an old seventeen. She was young for thirty-five. We would double-date—not just with these two. We saw all kinds of men. Never for very long, though. Three dates was about the record, because Mom would decide by the second evening out that there was something fishy—that her fellow was married, or running from somebody.

So it was perfectly fine with me. But I knew she hadn't pulled the plug on the evening because of my school, or the hour. I was late for school almost every day. Mom would say, "Why don't you wait and go in at noon? That would look better, not like we overslept, but more like you were ill. I'll write a note that says so."

As for studying, it was my practice to wait until the night before a test to read the books I was supposed to have read.

And I was used to a late schedule because of my waitress job, and the stars, and the late movies. If there was a scary movie on, one with a mummy or a prowler, say, Mom had to watch it, and she made me stay up to watch it with her.

"THANKS FOR THE GREEK FOOD AND FOR RIDING US around. Thank you for the beer," we said to our dates. We had been let out on our front sidewalk.

"Next time we won't take you to such a dive," said one of the men.

"Adios!" I called to them. I threw an arm around Mom.

"Until never," she said, as she waved.

We lived about ten miles north of Terre Haute—me, my mom, and my grandfather. We rented a stone house that was a regular Indiana-type house, on Burnside Boulevard, in a town called Phoenicia.

"Greater Metropolitan Phoenicia," my grandfather liked to say, the joke being that the whole town was really just two rows of shopping blocks on either side of I88.

Grandpa was up, in the living room. We were all night owls. He was having tea, and he had on the robe that was embroidered with dandelions, in honor of spring, I suppose.

"Girls," he greeted us. "Something called *The Creeper* on Channel Nine. Starring an Onslow Stevens. Nineteen forty-eight. Sounds like your sort of poison."

"Did you tell Lindy about our croquettes?" Mom asked him, and laughed. She tossed her handbag onto the couch and pushed up the sleeves of her sweater.

"I forgot all about telling Lindy about the croquettes. That totally slipped from my mind," Grandpa said.

"Well, honey, they poisoned Pop's chicken croquettes. They got his *dinner*," Mom said to me.

"A narrow escape," Grandpa said.

Lately it had been poison Mom talked about, and who knew if she was kidding? She also talked about "light pills" a great deal.

"This *Creeper* that's on—it says in the *Messenger*—he's half man, half cat-beast," Grandpa said.

"Ooh," Mom said, interested.

I asked them, "Would you like to go out in the back yard with me? I'll set up my telescope and show you some stuff."

I had a Frankus reflector telescope I bought with my waitress money. It wasn't perfect. I got it cheap. It did have motor drive, however, and a stabile equatorial mount, cradle rings, and engraved setting circles.

Mom and Grandpa said no, as always. Not that they could have told the difference between Ursa Minor and Hunting Dogs, but I wanted them, just once, to see how I could pull down Jupiter.

IT WAS LATE THE NEXT NIGHT, FRIDAY. I WAS IN MY uniform and shoes, just off from work. The big concern, whenever someone giant-stepped over my legs, which were propped up on the coffee table, was to protect my expensive support hose.

The job I had was on the dinner shift, five to eleven, at the Steak Chateau, Friday and Saturday evenings. Waitressing and bussing tables—I did both—could really wear you down. That evening I had been stiffed by a group of five adult people. That means no tip; a lot of juggling and running for nothing. Also, I had forgotten to charge one man for his chef's salad, and guess who got to pay for it.

Allen Tashman and Jay Gordon, accountants, were there at our place for popcorn and the Friday-night movie—one called *White Zombie.* They were there when I got home. Allen, the wimpy one, natch, I managed to talk into the back yard.

"Over that mass of shrubs by the garage. See?"

"I see," he said.

"The big Joe is Capella, eye of the Charioteer. And the Pleiades is hanging around somewhere in the same vicinity—there you go. Six little clots."

"Whoopee," he said.

But I loved telling them that stuff, although sometimes I was guessing, or making it up. I was just a C student in school.

"Hey, Lindy, by the way," Allen said, "are people stealing cars, that you know of?"

"Sis?" I asked. Mom and I were pretending to be sisters again.

"Yeah, she told me she thinks there's a car-theft ring in Phoenicia going on."

"Maybe there is," I said.

"She told me to park deep in the driveway and not out by the curb. Have you heard about it? A bunch of cars missing, from this neighborhood, way out here?"

"It's strange," I said, as if it could have been possible.

"I think your sister's crazy sometimes," Allen said.

I didn't bother to get the telescope. Oddly enough, on a *clear* night such as that, a star would have "boiled" in the viewfinder. The stars were too bright, was the problem. They were swimming in their own illumination.

WE WERE TALKING ABOUT BREAKFAST, WHICH NO-body wanted to fix. The weekend was over and it was Monday morning, getting on toward nine o'clock. I had intended to shake out of bed early, to see Venus in the west as a morning star. But Mom did something to my alarm clock.

She had been sleeping with me, the nights she got to sleep, in the same room, in the same bed.

She may have bashed my clock.

She probably reached over me and cuffed it.

So we were running behind. But I knew if I didn't eat breakfast I'd get queasy. "Make me an egg, please, Grandpa?"

"Poof, you're an egg. *I* made the coffee," he said.

"Mom, then. Please?"

She said, "Lindy, I can't, honey. I've got to look for my pills. Have either of you seen them anywhere, I wonder?"

"Not I, said the pig," said my grandfather.

"Sorry," I said.

"That's peculiar. Didn't I leave them with the vitamins?" Mom said. "This is important, you two."

"Nobody's got your medicine. Your medicine's not here," Grandpa said, causing Mom to be defensive.

"Never mind. I remember where they are," she said.

I doubted it, I really did. I doubted such things as "light pills" existed. Whenever she brought them up, I pictured something like a planet, boiling white—a radiant pill. I pictured Mom swallowing those! At the pharmacy, when she was haunting them, fretting around the prescription desk, they told her they didn't know what she was talking about, but if they did have such pills, she'd need a doctor's order.

"Just eat a banana. You'll be tardy again, Lindy," Grandpa said to me. "Harriet, they're going to fire you so fast if you waltz in late."

"I quit, Pop. They didn't like me there, so I quit," Mom said. That was the first we had heard of it.

Mom was a comptometer operator, and even though her mind was usually wandering over in Andromeda, she was one of the fastest operators in the state. She could get another job.

Grandpa had enough money for us, so that wasn't the worry. He had been a successful tailor, had even had his own shop. His only fault had been that he sometimes forgot to tie off his threads—so eventually, some of the clothes he made fell apart a little bit, or so he said.

The problem I saw was that Mom really needed to keep occupied.

Grandpa and she were still debating over who was going to fix breakfast when I stuffed my backpack and left for school.

Our landlady—she was nice—was on the cement porch steps next door where she lived. "Hey, Carl Sagan! Give me a minute!" she called, and I obliged. She said, "A Mrs. H. of Phoenicia asks: 'Why was there a ring around the moon last night?'"

"Ice crystals," I told her, thinking that was probably wrong.

"Goodness, I didn't realize it was that chilly," she said.

"Very high up," I said, still guessing.

It wasn't just our landlady. A lot of the neighbors knew me, and knew what a star fiend I was. They'd stop me and ask questions, like, "When is it we're getting Halley's Comet again?" Or, "What'd you make of the Saturn pictures?"

I never had to worry about security. When I was younger, for instance, when my mom wanted to go out, she would drop me way down the street at the movie theater. Then, a few times, either because I had sat through a second showing in order to resee my favorite parts, or because Mom accidentally forgot and didn't pick me up, I had to walk home in the dark. I didn't think a thing of it. There were these chummy neighbors all along the way.

"CAN'T WE GET OUT OF HERE? WHEN CAN WE GO?" Mom was asking me.

It was a couple days later, a Wednesday afternoon. I had been extended on the sofa, my head sandwiched between throw pillows so I wouldn't have to hear her carp. Our ironing board was set up—a nosy storky bird—aimed at me and waiting for me to press my uniform and something to wear to school the next day.

"Come on, Lindy," Mom urged me. "I need for you to explain to them."

She meant at the pharmacy.

Her good looks were going, I decided. Her brown hair was faded, and since she had quit work, she hadn't been changing her clothes often enough. I planned to iron a fresh something for her, and see if she'd wear it.

"Do you have to do that? Before we can leave?" she said, whining almost. I was testing the nozzle of the spray-starch can.

"What would happen if you didn't get some pills?" I asked her.

"I'd run out," she said, and shrugged.

First I did the collar on my uniform, which was a gingham check and not French-looking, as it ought to have been for a place called the "Chateau" anything.

"And then what would happen? After you ran out," I asked Mom.

"Honey," she said, and with a sigh, "I just should have told you. I should've told you *and* Pop. I have a little tumor. Like a tumor, and it's high up in my brain. I can't sleep well because of it, and I need sleep, or it'll worsen and be too diminishing, you see. But the pills fix me right up, is all they do. They give me a recharge. That's how you can think of it. So I don't need to sleep as much."

I finished ironing my uniform. I folded it and put it into a shopping bag so I could take it to school with me on Friday and keep it in my locker. Friday was going to be hell, I knew. There was a school tea planned for the morning, and in the afternoon I would graduate. Friday evening, the Chateau Jimmy was expecting to get crowds and crowds of seniors and their families.

Grandpa came in from the kitchen. His glasses were on from reading his newspaper. He wiggled a hand through the wrinkled clothes in my laundry basket, which rested on the couch.

"Tell him about your brain tumor, Mom," I said.

"Yeah, brain tumor," Grandpa said. "It's sinusitis. It's just from goldenrod."

It was like him to say that. If I ever had a headache, I got it from combing my hair too roughly, or parting it on the wrong side, according to him. He sat down in his chair. It was a maize color, and had heavy arms. "How does one called *The Magician* sound? It's the Fright Theatre feature this weekend."

I was thinking that Grandpa was a happier man when my father was around. I could completely forget about my father, these days, unless I was reminded. He had moved to Toledo, several years before, with his company. He had remarried. When he was still with us, though, he and my grandfather would trade jokes, and they'd make the *telling* of the joke last a long long time, which was the funniest part. Springs and summers, they would take Mom to the trotting races over at Geronimo Downs. They'd go almost nightly, in a white and red convertible they had between them.

IT WAS THURSDAY, THE MORNING BEFORE GRADUA-tion. I was cutting school, since it was nothing, just a rehearsal, and getting class rings and individual awards at an assembly—class artist, class-reunion secretary—not anything that involved me. I planned to show up after lunch and maybe pick up my cap and gown.

Mom and I were on the Shopper's Special, a bus that ran from Phoenicia to Terre Haute on weekdays. I hoped Mom was going to get her hair done, or buy an outfit for tomorrow, but she hadn't said she would. The other shoppers on the Special were a couple of lumpy women and a leather man in golfing clothes, and a guy in a maroon suit who had Mom's whole attention.

The bus shuddered at a light. Its engine noise and the tremor in the hard seat and the clear early sun were all getting to me, making me drowsy.

The maroon suit was behind a Chicago newspaper. Mom glanced back at him. "What do you think *he* does?" she asked me.

"Could be anything," I said.

"No, kiddo. That's a plainclothesman. You can tell."

"He could be," I said.

"He is. I believe he's on here for us."

I was very used to this talk, but today I didn't feel like hearing it. "Please," I said to Mom.

"Forget it," she said.

She looked young again. "Don't act up, girls," the bus driver had teased us when we got on in Phoenicia.

"I can do something," I said to Mom. "I can name the fifteen brightest stars. Want me to? I can give them in order of brightness."

Mom seemed stunned by the offer and her face slackened. The concern went out of her eyes. She looked twelve. "Can you do something like that? Did you have to learn it in school, or on your own?"

"*I* did it. Here we go. They are Sirius, Canopus, Alpha Centauri, Arcturus, Vega," I told her, and right on through to old reddish Antares.

Mom was both smiling and grave, like a person hearing a favorite poem.

"Mom," I said, after a minute, "before commencement tomorrow, there's the Senior Tea. It's just cookies and junk, but I told them maybe you'd help serve. They wanted parents to be guards for the tables, just so nobody takes a hundred cookies instead of one or two."

She was surprised, I could tell. I wondered if she was flattered that I wanted her to be there.

"Honey, I couldn't do *that*," she said, as though I had asked her to leap over our garage, or jog to Kansas. "I couldn't do that."

The trip to Terre Haute was all the way beside a river. Sometimes, the river was just a large ditch and sometimes it was an actual wild river. Today, it was full to the banks, and we were rolling along in the bus at the same rate as the current.

In the corner of my sight, I saw Mom fussing with the jumbo purse she had brought. I peeked down into it, and there were her toothbrush and plastic soap box and her cloth hair-curlers. So I knew she was thinking of getting off at Platte and seeing if they had a bed for her at the Institute there. I thought maybe her Dr. Goff, whom she saw, had decided she ought to check in for a bit again. Or, more probably it was her idea.

THE HOSPITAL WAS MOM'S IDEA, I FINALLY LEARNED from Grandpa, but it turned out they didn't have space for her, or they didn't think she needed to get in right then.

She wasn't at my graduation ceremony, which was just as well, in one way—I didn't do a great job, since I had missed rehearsal. During the sitting moments, I wondered about her, though, and I decided that graduation had been one of the chief things upsetting her. She was scared of the "going forward into the world" parts of the commencement speeches.

Grandpa lied to me. He said he was certain Mom was there, just back in one of the cooler seats, under the buckeye trees. Graduation was outside, see. He said Mom wanted shade.

LATE THAT NIGHT, WE WERE ALL THREE WATCHING the Fright Theatre feature. A girl in the movie was married to a man who changed into a werewolf and attacked people. Sooner or later, you knew he was going to go after the girl.

"That poor woman," Mom kept saying.

"She's got it tough, all right," Grandpa said. "Trying to keep her husband in Alpo."

I was exhausted from work. I was nibbling the black kernels and oily salt from the bottom of the popcorn bowl.

"She has to make sure he's got all his shots. He's got to be wormed. Here she comes now, going to give him a flea collar," Grandpa said.

I liked being as dragged out as I was. My new apricot robe that Grandpa had made for me was across my legs, keeping them warm. My other graduation gifts, from Mom—really Grandpa—were all telescope related.

There was a pause in the movie for a commercial. "Take a reading on this," Grandpa said. He flipped a big white card to me. The card said, "Happy Graduation, Good Luck in Your Future." It had come from my dad.

I was still looking at the signature, *Your father,* when the movie started back up again. "What if Dad were back living with us?" I asked Grandpa and Mom.

"It would cut down on your mom's dating," Grandpa said.

Mom, concentrating on the television, said, "Uh oh, full moon!"

"But just suppose Dad were to somehow come back here and live with us," I said to Mom. I had put down the card and was pulling on my short hair a little.

"He better not," she said.

"You're damn right, he better not," Grandpa said.

I was surprised. He even sounded angry. I guessed I had been wrong, thinking Grandpa missed having Dad as a crony so much.

I stuffed a pillow behind my head and sat back and listened to the creepy music from the television and to a moth that was stupidly banging on the window screen. It would take a lot for my dad to understand us, and the way we three did things, I thought. He would have to do some thinking.

"Ah, this couch feels good!" I said. "I could lie here forever."

I didn't know whether or not Mom had heard me. But she was beaming, either way. She pointed to the TV screen, where the werewolf lay under a bush, becoming a person again. She said, "Shh."

The Wellman Twins

"YOU NEVER LIE TO ME," BLUEY WROTE BEFORE THE nose of his cedar pencil snapped. He shrugged, reread the page. He had meant to come off as someone firm, plain-minded, blunt; someone deliberate. He thought in the past he had too often seemed moony and fragile.

He was on his hip, on the discreet floor matting. He was comfortable, with his elbow buried in a cushion he had filched from the great couch. He lay near a box speaker—one of six that was wired into the house sound system. The song that raged was "Take Her," a twenty-minute song with locomotive rhythms, done by an English band called Island of Agathas.

Bluey thought the music might warm him into his new attitude.

He kept his writings, his "Letters to Ivy," in a loose binder that was now so fat you needed two wide rubber bands to keep it square and manageable. There were seventy letters, something in the region of five hundred sheets. He wanted to finish this latest one with a lie. But his pencil was broken and, besides, the lie was so ill-conceived it dissolved in Bluey's mind even as he was trying to frame it in words: "So I'll tell you. I've met a girl who is lovely, who is a model, who is much older, who is much younger, but wise, and a mermaid in the moonlit breakers. . . ."

There was noise at the front door—calling and banging. The family dog left his toy, a cherry-red plastic mouse, and went to answer. Bluey followed, shutting up the Island of Agathas as he passed the turntable.

He opened one of the double doors to Greer, his twin sister, whose arms were busy with a nylon tote, a cased viola, a bottle of champagne, and a fountain of sweet rocket—flowers that were fitted into a tissue-paper cone. She had knee-thumped the door.

"At last!" she said, and, "Guess what? Sixty-seven tax-free dollars I made! So there!"

"Yeah, but you spent it on flowers and wine, right?" Bluey said.

"Up yours," Greer said.

She was a street musician, or had been recently. She played to the lunch crowds in Newport. This was instead of having a real summer job, though neither twin had to work just yet. They were provided for by their mother, who was provided for by the life insurance, the stock portfolio, and the investment planning of her late husband, the twins' father. He was Wellman of Wellman's Valve in Kingston, Rhode Island. He had never seen his children. He had died during his wife's pregnancy.

The twins were one-month alumni of U.R.I., where they had graduated without honors, but had both been pre-med, and had both been accepted at University of Maine's medical school.

"You're not really wearing all that eyebrow makeup. Tell me I'm seeing things," Bluey said.

"Lemme by," Greer said. "Goddamn it, Deuce, stop!"

Deuce the retriever was bounding at Greer. Bluey hooked the dog's choke collar with a finger and took the champagne bottle from his sister with his free hand. He let Greer pass, though he gave her a look of impatience.

Greer went right, to the kitchen.

Bluey tapped the dog's flat head very lightly with the bottle. "You get peaceful, I'm warning," Bluey said, and then loosed the dog and went Greer's way.

SHE WAS WHISTLING, ALREADY STACKING TOGETHER a sandwich of raw vegetables on protein bread.

"What do you do, comb your hair with a scissors?" Bluey said. "And what's with the survival wear?"

Greer was in a shirt with a camouflage pattern. The shirt had deep pockets and long sleeves that were turned back in big rolls over her delicate arms.

"Is that sandwich for you? It looks like rodent food. It looks like you're making it for a gerbil or a ground chuck."

Greer said, "You don't mean a ground chuck. Where's the clover honey, please? Ground chuck is meat. You mean a wood-chuck or a groundhog. Maybe a hedgehog."

"I mean it looks too dry for a human being to swallow— and, wow, will Mother do a back flip when she sees your *hair*."

The twins' mother was having her summer in Hawaii, in a time-share condo she had bought into.

"Are you listening at all, Greer?"

"Go be someplace else. Give me my booze," Greer said.

Bluey did, but said, "You're lucky you're still young. Soon

your body won't be able to metabolize these ungodly amounts of alcohol."

"Oh, spare us. I'm allowed to celebrate."

Bluey remembered the letter he had been writing and hurried to put it away.

Deuce was in the parlor, coiled on the center seat of the mammoth couch. "You're not serious," Bluey said to him. Deuce beat his tail and ducked his head.

"Leave *him* alone, too!" Greer shouted.

Bluey took his notebook and new pages to his room—what had once been his father's study and at-home office. The walls were tacked over with blank watercolor paper, which was Bluey's idea, and the furniture was white-painted cane. Matchstick blinds screened the window light. Bluey propped a side chair under the knob of his lockless door.

DEUCE WAS ALLOWING HIS HAUNCHES TO BE USED AS a pillow for Greer's head. They were on the sofa—both drunk, Bluey decided.

"Good. Savor the fruits of your labor. I am jealous, I guess. Not about the money, but of the nerve you must have to stand up and perform in front of an audience. Real people who can react—good or bad—right there to your face. Did you give Deuce some Mumm's?"

"Oui," Greer said.

"Congratulations on the sixty-seven dollars," Bluey said.

"Who's this different person from an hour ago, Deuce? Do we know this guy?" Greer asked the dog.

"I like your clothes, too. I like the fatigue pants," Bluey said.

Greer did a leg raise. "These pants fought in the D.M.Z."

"Aha," Bluey said.

"Also, did you know Deuce has a girly friend? Yes, he does. She came calling while you were—whatever you were doing. Getting sweet. She's a demure red spaniel."

"Unh," said Bluey, sounding defeated and far away.

"Say, if you're at loose ends . . ." Greer said.

"No, I just feel weird."

"Well, I was going to suggest you build a nice hangover like me and Deuce are doing. It's all right. We're twenty-one, all of us."

THE SKY HAD PINKED UP NICELY IN THE WEST, WAS going gray in the east. The twins were on the high back deck, playing canasta on a picnic bench with X-shaped legs. The view behind them, over a kind of porch of leaves, was of nice houses like theirs.

The next lawn was big like a playing field, and it tilted steeply down. A bare-chested man was fighting the grade, shoving a green mower. His shirt was tied to the mower's handlebars.

"That's Bing," Greer told Bluey. "Bing Litzinger and his grinding machine kept me from napping, and not only that but Buh-Buh-Bing will get all the insects moving from over there to over here. Yes, he will. Triste but true."

"Knock off the French," Bluey said.

"Oh, no, Deuce, Bluey the crank is back. Hey, where is Deuce?"

"I let him run," Bluey said.

Greer jumped from the table, went indoors, and was gone for a while. Bluey, wearing only swim trunks and a baseball cap, shuffled the cards as if they could warm him. He heard his sister's shrieking whistle from the side of the house. Finally, Greer was back, carrying clothes.

"Dog's gone forever. Probably eloped," she said. "Here. These'll ruin your bad mood." She traded Bluey's cap for one of her straw picture hats. Its brim was enormous. She wrapped a long scarf at Bluey's neck, telling him, "You were cold." She draped his black blazer over his shoulders.

"God, I wish you'd sober down," he said.

"Paging Dr. Wellman," Greer said. "You're wanted in Pre-Op. Stat. Code Blue."

"Dr. Wellman, you're wanted in Detox," Bluey said.

Greer sat and dealt. As she fanned her cards, she nodded agreeably, acknowledging each one.

Bluey watched her, re-aimed his gaze, fidgeted. He said, "I'm sorry, I can't stand this." He plucked the straw hat off and sailed it over the deck rail. "Why am I so jittery?"

"It's all right," Greer said. "We'll get bold. I've got some great things stored away."

Getting bold was the twins' name—a name thought up when they were younger—for a session of truth-telling.

"Let's crowd the last available boundaries of decency and privacy," Greer said.

"Yeah, trample 'em," said Bluey.

"Okay, I'll start. I read your letters to Ivy," Greer said. "Good start?" she added after a minute.

Bluey kept a long silence, and his eyes, Greer could see even in the dimming light, blinked too much.

"Well, I'll never forgive you. I can't imagine forgiving you," he said at last.

"Naturally. Way to play."

Bluey said, "I've got to get Deuce."

"I'll wait. No, change that. I'll wait inside," Greer said.

Bluey went barefooted down the deck steps, walking a little sideways to avoid splinters. He ducked through a five-tree orchard of crab apple his father had once devised.

Bluey was slapping at mosquitoes when he saw the flash of the dog's silky coat, and then he saw Deuce pile out of tall grass and galumph into Bing Litzinger's yard. The dog lifted himself onto the birdbath there and drank.

Bluey was sneaking up on him when Litzinger, who had finished mowing, came from his house.

"Get him out!" Litzinger called.

"I'm trying, damn it," Bluey said. The dog bucked at the sound of Bluey's voice and sprinted in a meaningless circle.

"There's a leash law. I can't have a dog in the yard," Litzinger said. He watched the contest as Bluey tried to capture Deuce. The dog was taunting, getting just beyond reach, his butt raised up, his front legs flat on the grass.

"I know your mother," Litzinger warned before heading back to his house.

GREER WAS IN THE KITCHEN, WEARING THE PICTURE hat that she said she had climbed over the deck to retrieve. She was eating a bran muffin and a cup of lemon yogurt.

Bluey had dragged Deuce with him. The dog's nails scraped on the polished floor. His tail was stuffed down, his ears back.

"You're *still* purple with rage," Greer said to Bluey. "Why don't you crash a dish or two?"

Bluey freed the dog, straightened, removed a brandy bottle from a cupboard. The ship calendar on the cupboard door flapped. Bluey measured out a full glass. "They do this in movies," he said, and tried to drink it all. He couldn't manage even a full swallow.

"They probably have their stand-ins do it," Greer said.

Bluey gasped and breathed for a bit. He said, "Okay, where were we? Ivy, the girl I write to, I met at an Iggy Pop concert. You couldn't know her; she didn't go to school with us. She lives in Boston. We were both high when we met. I, you know, liked her. Really, tremendous . . ."

"Got it," Greer said.

"I thought we were high. So we agreed, after that night, we'd keep in touch. Next day, phone call from her. I was very flattered. But the thing being, she *wasn't* high the night before. She's always like that. Babbling. She's probably got maybe a brain tumor or a limbic disorder. She thinks her brother had something to do with killing Lennon. That kind of thing. I mean, I liked her for her looks, but what's the use?"

"Bluey, this all sounds like a lie. One of your lies," Greer said.

"So who I'm writing to is sort of Ivy, but sort of not, and what would be the point of mailing the letters? Most of all, they're for me."

"Well, that's a violently unpleasant story if it's true," Greer said in a summarizing tone. "Now. What've you got to crush me with?"

The dog, under the table, charged Greer's shoe—a pale moccasin. She crossed her ankles in halfhearted defense.

"Nothing," Bluey said.

"Don't be cruel," Greer said.

"I have nothing for you. Live with that one, Greer."

"Go ahead and gnaw off the whole heel. What the hell," Greer said to Deuce.

"Except this," Bluey said. "Mom told it to me, though it doesn't mean much. You were not expected. You were not prepared for. Your body was behind mine—in the womb, I mean. Shadowing mine. Our father died and never even knew you were there. Now I'm sorry I told you," Bluey said.

"No, don't be. I think it's interesting what's going on. You hoped I'd feel unwanted?"

"Somewhat. To pay you back for reading my letters," Bluey said.

"My, my," Greer said, and sighed.

Eventually she said, "I don't think you're playing this game well at all, Bluey. I mean, I don't know which lie is bigger—Ivy of Boston or the shadow in the womb."

"Hey," Bluey said, alarmed.

"Or *my* lie. I never read your letters. Relax. I never saw them but for the 'Letters to Ivy' title."

"You didn't read them? Never even looked through them?"

"Nope," Greer said.

"Well, someday you were going to get to. You were supposed to," Bluey said.

"Look at what the moonlight's doing to the grape trellis," Greer said. "Out the window."

"You hear me? The letters are to you," Bluey said.

"You didn't have anyone else to write to?" Greer said. She touched her sternum.

"No one else to write to," Bluey echoed.

Greer pressed back in her chair seat, her neck stiffening. She spoke slowly and purposefully, as though Bluey were a stranger. "Then I shall read them. Sometime. Whenever it is to your liking."

"No, forget it. I don't think so," Bluey said.

"Well, were you sort of kidding about their being written to me?" Greer asked.

"They aren't to anybody, really. Or they're to every girl. Only I don't deeply know any other girl. They're to a fantasy I have in my brain."

"Aw, Bluey, wait awhile," Greer said. "Lots of things could change for you. It doesn't seem like it, but they've got to, don't they?" Greer said. "Don't they?"

Coach

THE AUGUST TWO-A-DAY PRACTICE SESSIONS WERE sixty-seven days away, Coach calculated. He was drying breakfast dishes. He swabbed a coffee cup and made himself listen to his wife, who was across the kitchen, sponging the stove's burner coils.

"I know I'm no Rembrandt," Sherry said, "but I have so damn much fun trying, and this little studio—this room—we can afford. I could get out of your way by going there and get you and Daphne out of my way. No offense."

"I'm thinking," Coach said.

His wife coasted from appliance to appliance. She swiped the face of the oven clock with her sponge. "You're thinking too slow. Your reporter's coming at nine and it's way after eight now. Should I give them a deposit on the studio or not? Yes or no?"

Coach was staring at the sink, at a thread of water that came from one of the taps. He thought of the lake place where they used to go in North Carolina. He saw green water being thickly sliced by a power boat; the boat towing Sherry, who was blonde and laughing on her skis, her rounded back strong, her suit shining red.

"Of course, of course, give them the money," he said.

Their daughter, Daphne, wandered into the kitchen. She was dark-haired, lazy-looking, fifteen. Her eyes were lost behind bangs. She drew open the enormous door of the refrigerator.

"Don't hang, Daphne, you'll unhinge things," her mother said. "What are you after?"

"Food mainly," Daphne said.

Sherry went away, to the little sun patio off the kitchen. Coach pushed the glass door sideways after her and it smacked shut.

"Eat and run," he said to Daphne. "I've got a reporter coming in short order. Get dressed." He spoke firmly but in the smaller voice he always used for his child.

"Yes, sir," Daphne said. She broke into the freezer compartment and ducked to let its gate pass over her head. "Looks bad. Nothing in here but Eggos."

"I ate Eggos. Just hustle up," Coach said.

"Can I be here for this guy?" Daphne asked.

"Who guy? The reporter? Nuh-uh. He's just from the college, Daph. Coming to see if the new freshman coach has three heads or just two."

Daphne was nodding at the food jars racked on the wide refrigerator door. "Hey, lookit," she said. She blew a breath in front of the freezer compartment and made a short jet of mist.

Coach remembered a fall night, a Friday-game night, long ago, when he had put Daphne on the playing field. It was during the ceremonies before his unbeaten squad had taken on Ignatius South. High School. Parents' Night. He had laced shoulder pads on Daphne and draped the trainer's gag jersey—number 1/2—over her, and balanced Tim-somebody's helmet on her eight-year-old head. She was lost in the getup, a small pile of equipment out on the fifty-yard line. She had applauded when the loudspeaker announced her name, when the p. a. voice, garbled by amplification and echo, had rung out, "Daughter of our coach, Harry Noonan, and his wife—number one-half, Daphne Noonan!" She had stood in the bath of floodlights, shaking as the players and their folks strolled by—the players grim in their war gear, the parents tiny and apologetic-seeming in civilian clothes. The co-captain of the team, awesome in his pads and cleats and steaming from warm-up running, had palmed Daphne's big helmet and twisted it sideways. From behind, from the home stands, Coach had heard, "Haaa!" as Daphne turned circles of happy confusion, trying to right the helmet. Through the ear hole her left eye had twinkled, Coach remembered. He had heard, "God, that's funny," and "Coach's kid."

ON THE SUN PORCH NOW, HIS WIFE WAS DOING A SET of tennis exercises. She was between Coach and the morning sun, framed by the glass doors. He could see through the care-less weave of her caftan, enough to make out the white flesh left by her swimsuit.

"I knew you wouldn't let me," Daphne said. She had poured a glass of chocolate milk. She pulled open a chilled banana. "I bet Mom gets to be here."

"Daph, this isn't a big deal. We've been through it all be-fore," Coach said.

"Not for a college paper," Daphne said. "Wait a minute, I'll be right back." She left the kitchen.

"I'll hold my breath and count the heartbeats," Coach said to the space she had left behind.

They were new to the little town, new to Pennsylvania. Coach was assuming charge of the freshman squad, in a league where freshmen weren't eligible for the varsity. He had taken the job, not sure if it was a step up for him or a serious misstep. The money was so-so. But he wanted the college setting for his family—especially for Daphne. She had been seeming to lose interest in the small celebrity they achieved in high-school towns. She had acted bored at the Noonans' Sunday spaghetti dinners for standout players. She had stopped fetching plates of food for the boys, who were too game-sore to get their own. She had even stopped wearing the charm bracelet her parents had put together for her—a silver bracelet with a tiny megaphone, the numerals 68—a league championship year—and, of course, a miniature football.

Coach took a seat at the kitchen table. He ate grapes from a bowl. He spilled bottled wheat germ into his palm. On the table were four chunky ring binders, their black leatherette covers printed with the college seal—which still looked strange to him. These were his playbooks, and he was having trouble getting the play tactics into his head.

"Will you turn off the radio?" he yelled.

The bleat from Daphne's upstairs bedroom ceased. A minute later she came down and into the kitchen. She had a cardboard folder and some textbooks with her. "Later on, would you look at this stuff and help me? Can you do these?" she asked Coach.

He glanced over one of her papers. It was penciled with algebra equations, smutty with erasures and scribbled-out parts. "I'd have to see the book, but no. Not now, not later. I don't want to and I don't have time."

"That's just great," Daphne said.

"Your mother and I got our algebra homework done already, Daph. We turned ours in," Coach said. "This was in nineteen fifty-six."

"Mom!" Daphne said, pushing aside the glass door.

"Forget it," Sherry said.

2

TOBY, THE BOY SENT FROM *THE ROOTER* TO INTER-view Coach, was unshaven and bleary-eyed. He wore a rumpled cerise polo shirt and faded Levi's. He asked few questions, dragging his words. Now and then he grumbled of a hangover and no sleep. He yawned during Coach's answers. He took no notes.

"You're getting this now?" Coach said.

"Oh, yeah, it's writing itself, I'm such a pro," Toby said, and Coach wasn't certain if the boy was kidding.

"So, you've been here just a little while. Lucky you," Toby said. "Less than a month?"

"Is that like a question? It seems less than less than a month—less than a week—a day and a half," Coach said.

For the interview, he had put on white sports slacks and a maroon pullover with a gold collar—the college's colors. The pullover he had bought at Campus World. The clothes had a snug fit that flattered Coach and showed off his flat stomach and heavy biceps.

He and Toby were on either end of the sofa in the living room of the house, a wooden two-story Coach had found and would be paying off for decades, he was sure.

Toby said, "Well, believe it or not, I've got enough for a couple sticks, which is shoptalk among we press men for two columns. If you're going to be home tomorrow, there's a girl who'll come and take your picture—Marcia. She's a drag, I warn you."

"One thing about this town, there aren't any damn sidewalks, and the cars don't give you much room if you're jogging," Coach said, standing up.

"Hey, tell me about it. When I'm hitching, I wear an orange safety poncho and carry a red flag and paint a big X on my back. Of course, I'm probably just making a better target," the reporter said.

"I jog down at the track now. It's a great facility, comparable to a Big Ten's. I like the layout," Coach said.

"Okay, but the interview's over," Toby said.

"Well, I came from high schools, remember. In Indiana and Ohio—good schools with good budgets, mind you, but high schools, nonetheless."

"Yeah, I got where you're coming from," Toby said.

"Did you need to know what courses I'll be handling? Fall quarter, they've got me lined up for two things: The Atlantic World is the first one, and Colloquium on European Industrial Development, I think it is. Before, I always taught World History. P.O.D., once or twice."

"That three-eighty-one you're going to teach is a tit course, in case nobody's informed you. It's what we call lunch," Toby said.

"It's, in nature, a refresher class," Coach said.

"Yeah, or out of nature," Toby said.

DAPHNE CAME FROM THE LONG HALL STEPS INTO the living room. Her dark hair was brushed and lifting with static. Her eyes seemed to Coach larger than usual, and a little sooty around the lashes.

"You're just leaving, aren't you, buster?" Coach said to her.

"Retrieving a pencil," Daphne said.

"Is your name really Buster?" Toby asked.

"Get your pencil and scoot. This is Toby here. Toby, this is my daughter, Daphne," Coach said.

"Nice to meet you," Daphne said. She slipped into a deep chair at the far corner of the long living room.

"Can she hear us over in that county?" Toby said. "Do you read me?" he shouted.

Daphne smiled. Coach saw bangs and her very white teeth.

"Come on, Daph, hit the trail," he said.

"I've got a joke for her first," Toby said. "What's green and moves very fast?"

"Frog in a blender," Daphne said. "Dad? Some friends invited me to go swimming with them at the Natatorium. May I?"

"You've got to see the Nat. It's the best thing," Toby said.

"What about your class, though? She's in makeup school here, Toby, catching up on some algebra that didn't take the first time around."

Toby wrinkled his nose at Daphne. "At first, I thought you meant *makeup* school, like lipstick and rouge."

"I wish," Daphne said.

She slipped her left foot from her leather sandal and casually stroked the toes.

"She's a nut for swimming," Coach said.

"You'll be so bored here. Most nights, your options are either ordering a pizza or slashing your wrists," Toby told Daphne.

"Oh," she said, rolling her chin on her shoulder in a rather seductive way.

"Take it from Toby," he said.

Coach let Toby through the front door, and watched until he was down the street.

"He was nice," Daphne said.

"Aw, Daph. That's what you say about everybody. There's a lot better things you could say—more on-the-beam things."

"I guess you're mad," she said.

Coach went to the kitchen, to sit down with his play-books again. Daphne came after him.

"Aren't you?" she said.

"I guess you thought he was cute," Coach said. He flapped through some mimeographed pages, turning them on the notebook's silver rings. "I don't mean to shock you about it, but you'd be wasting your time there, Daph. You'd be trying to start a fire with a wet match."

Daphne stared at her father. "That's sick!" she said.

"I'm not criticizing him for it. I'm just telling you," Coach said.

3

"THIS IS COMPLETELY WRONG," COACH SAID SADLY. He read further. "Oh, no," he said. He drowned the newspaper in his bath water and slogged the pages over into a corner by the commode.

His wife handed him a dry edition, one of the ten or twelve *Rooters* Daphne had brought home.

Sherry was parallel to Coach on the edge of the tub, sitting with her back braced against the wall. "Oh, cheer up," she said. "Nobody reads a free newspaper."

Coach quartered the dry *Rooter* into a package around Toby's article. "Well, I wasn't head coach at Elmgrove, and I sure wasn't Phi Beta Kappa. And look at this picture," Coach said.

"What's so wrong with it?" Sherry said.

"Where did he get that you were at Mt. Holyoke? And I didn't bitch about the sidewalks this much."

"You didn't?" Sherry said. "That's almost too bad. I thought that was the best part of the article."

Coach slunk farther into the warm water until it crowded his chin. He kept the newspaper aloft. "Oh, come on, give me some credit here! Don't they have any supervision over in Journalism? I don't see how he could get away with this shit. It's an unbelievably sloppy job."

"It's just a dinky article in a handout paper, Coach. What do you care? It wouldn't matter if he said we were a bright-green family with scales," Sherry said.

"He didn't think of that or he would have. This breaks my heart," Coach said.

"Daph liked it," Sherry said.

Coach wearily chopped bath water with the side of his hand and threw a splash at the soap recess in the tiled wall. "I tell you, I'm going to be spending my whole first year here explaining how none of it's true."

"What difference does true make?" Sherry said.

4

COACH WAS SEATED AWKWARDLY ON AN IRON STOOL at a white table on the patio of the Dairy Frost. Daphne was across from him, fighting the early evening heat for her mocha-fudge cone. She tilted her head at the cone, lapping at it.

"You aren't saying anything," Coach said.

"Wait," Daphne said.

She worked on the cone.

"I've been waiting."

"If you two want to separate, it's none of my business," she said.

They were facing the busy parking lot when a new Pontiac turned in off the highway, glided easily onto the gravel, took a parking slot close by. In the driver's seat was a boy with built-up shoulders—a boy who looked very familiar to Coach. In back was a couple in their fifties—the boy's parents, Coach thought—both talking at once.

"Have I been spilling all this breath for nothing? *Not* a separation," Coach said. "Not anything like it."

"All right, not," Daphne said. She stopped in her attack on the cone long enough to watch the Pontiac boy step out. Dark brown ice cream streamed between her knuckles and down the inside of her wrist.

"You're losing it, honey," Coach said.

Daphne dabbed around the cone and her hand, making repairs.

"Hell, *real* trouble your father wouldn't tell you about at a *Dairy* Frost. This apartment your mom found is like an office or something. A studio for her to go to and get away every now and then. That kid's in my backfield. What the *hell's* his name?"

They watched as the young man took orders from his parents, then went inside the Dairy Frost. He looked both wider and taller than the other patrons, out of their scale. His rump and haunches were thick with muscle. His neck was fat but tight.

"Bobby Stark!" Coach said, and smiled very quickly at the parents in the Pontiac. He turned back to his daughter.

"She wants to get away from us," Daphne said.

"Definitely not. She gave me a list, is how this whole thing started. She's got stuff she wants to do, and you with your school problems and me with the team—we're too much for her, see? She could spend her entire day on us, if you think about it, and never have one second for herself. If you think about it fairly, Daphne, you'll agree."

Daphne seemed to consider. She was focused on the inside of the Dairy Frost building, and for a while she kept still.

"That guy looks dumb. One of the truly dumb," she said.

"My halfback? He's not. He was his class salutatorian," Coach said.

"He doesn't know *you*."

"Just embarrassed," Coach said. "Can we stick to the point,

Daph? And quit rocking the boat. Look what you're doing."
Daphne's arm was on the table and she was violently swinging
her legs under her chair.

She made a sigh and marched over to a trash can to deposit
her slumping cone. Then she washed up at the children's drinking fountain and rejoined Coach, who had finished his Brown
Cow but had kept the plastic spoon in his mouth.

"What was on this list of Mom's?" Daphne asked.

"Adult stuff," Coach said.

"Just give me an example."

Coach removed the plastic spoon and cracked it in half.

"Your mother's list is for five years. In that time, she wants
to be speaking French regularly. She wants to follow up on her
printmaking."

"This is adult stuff?" Daphne said.

Coach raised a hand to Bobby Stark. Stark had three malt
cups in a cardboard carrier and he was moving toward the parking lot.

"Hey, those all for you?" Coach called out.

"I got a month to get fat, Coach. You'll have five months to
beat it off me," the boy called back.

The people at some of the tables around Coach's lit up with
grins. Bobby Stark's parents were grinning.

"Every hit of that junk takes a second off your time in the
forty—just remember that!" Coach shouted.

Stark wagged his head ruefully, his cheeks blushing. He
pretended to hide the malts behind his arm.

"Duh," Daphne said in a hoarse voice. "Which way to
the door, Coach?"

"He can hear you," Coach said.

"Duh, kin I have a candy bar, Coach?" she rasped.

They faced Stark, who smiled a little crookedly at Daphne, and threw her a wink so dazzling, she went silent.

5

COACH WAS IN THE BASEMENT LAUNDRY ROOM, BOTH arms busy hugging a bundle of jogging clothes. He was waiting on the washer, waiting for Sherry to unload her clothes.

"The Cowboys are soaking their players in a sense-deprivation tub of warm saltwater," she said.

"We know," Coach said.

"If Dallas is doing it, I just thought you might want to consider it."

"We have. Hustle up a little with your stuff, will you?" Coach said.

"It's like my apartment," Sherry said. "A place apart."

Coach cut her off. "Don't go on about how much you love your apartment."

"I wasn't going to," Sherry said. She slung her wet slacks and blouses into the dryer.

Coach had just two weeks before the start of the heavy practices. His team would have him then, he knew, almost straight through to the Christmas holidays.

"I like that," Coach said. "A place apart."

A HALF HOUR LATER, COACH AND HIS WIFE WERE ON the side patio. They could hear the tick of the clothes dryer downstairs. Sherry had changed into a halter top. She was taking sun on her back, adding to her tan.

"You know what's odd?" she said. "Daphne's popularity here. I don't mean it's odd."

"She's always done terrific with people, always gone over well," Coach said.

"*Your* people, though. These are hers," Sherry said. "Like that reporter."

"Yeah, they're like sisters," Coach said.

6

IT WAS A WEEK BEFORE THE TWO-A-DAY PRACTICE sessions would begin. The sky was colorless and glazed, like milk glass. When Coach looked at the sun, his eyes ached, his head screamed.

He had run some wind sprints on the stadium field, and now he was doing an easy lap. A stopwatch on a noose of ribbon swung against his chest. He cut through the goalposts and trotted for the sidelines, for the twenty, where he had dumped his clipboard and a towel.

Someone called to him.

Blond Bobby Stark came out from under the stands. His football shoes were laced together and draped around his neck. He wore a midriff-cut T-shirt and shorts. He walked gingerly in white wool socks.

"Did everybody go? Or am I the first one here?" he called to Coach.

"'Bout a half hour," Coach said, heaving.

Stark sat down to untangle his shoes, and Coach, sweating, stood over him.

Coach spat. He folded his arms in a way that pushed out his muscles. He sniffed, twisting his whole nose and mouth to the left. He said, "You know, Stark, you were salutatorian for your class."

"High school," the boy said. He grinned up at Coach, an eye pinched against the glare.

"That counts, believe me. Maybe we can use you to help some of our slower players along—some of the linemen, maybe I'm thinking."

"What do you mean—tutor?" Stark said.

"Naw. Teach them to eat without biting off their fingers. How to tie a necktie. Some of your style," Coach said, and Stark bobbed his head.

Stark settled the fit of his right shoe. He said, "But there aren't any really dumb ones on our squad, because they'd just get flunked out. Recruiters won't touch them in this league. There wouldn't be any percentage in it."

"Then I'm greatly relieved," Coach said.

He planted his feet along a furrow of lime-eaten grass. He faced the open end of the stadium, where the enormous library building stood shimmering and uncertain behind sheets of heat that rose from the parking area.

Stark stood up and studied his shoes as he began jogging in place. He danced twenty yards down the field; loped back.

Other players were arriving for the informal session. Coach meant to time them in the mile, and in some dashes.

Stark looked jittery. He walked in semicircles, crowding Coach.

"What're you worried about?" Coach asked him. "Girl problems you got? You pull a muscle already?"

Stark glanced quickly around them. He said, "I live all my life two doors down from Coach Burton's house. My mom and Burton's wife are best friends, so I always know what's going on."

Burton had been the head coach of the varsity team for over a decade.

"You probably know about it already, anyway," Stark said. "Do you?"

"What the hell are you talking about, Stark?"

"You don't know? Typical. Burton's leaving, see? Like at the end of this year. His wife wants him out real bad, and the alumni want him out because they're tired of losing seasons. So what I heard was you were brought in because of it. And if we do okay this season, like you'll be varsity coach next year."

"That's conjecture," Coach said. But he was excited.

IT WAS THREE O'CLOCK, STILL HOT. COACH WAS moving along a sidewalk with Bobby Stark, who was balanced on a racing bicycle, moving just enough to keep the machine upright.

"Three things," Coach said. "I've seen all the game films from last year, and I came here personally and witnessed the Tech game. No one lost because of the coaching. A coach can work miracles with a good team, but he is *helpless* if his personnel don't want it bad enough. That's the worst part about running a team—you can't climb down into your people's hearts and change them."

Some college girls in a large expensive car went past. They shrieked and whistled at Bobby Stark.

"Lifeguards at the pool," he explained.

"I don't know if Burton's leaving or not," Coach continued. "But if his wife wants him to go, he probably will. If you're ever thinking about a career in coaching someday, Bob, think about that. Your family's either with you or you've had it. And remember, whether you stay someplace or not depends completely on a bunch of *kids*. I swear, I'd give up a leg for a chance to get in a game myself—just one play, with what I know now."

Stark nodded. They went on a block, and he said, "I turn off here. You going to tell your daughter about the job?"

"My daughter?" Coach said, and smiled.

7

NO ONE WAS HOME. A MAGNET UNDER A PLASTIC ladybug held a note to the face of the refrigerator. The note read:

Harry, I'm at my place. Daph's with Toby
K. somewhere, fooling around. Be good now,
Sherry Baby.

"Dope," Coach said.

He felt very good.

He took a beer upstairs and drank it while he showered. He cinched on a pair of sweat pants and, wearing only these, went back down and fetched another beer.

He watched some of a baseball game on cable. He thought

over his conversation with Bobby Stark. "Boy, is that true!" Coach said, and then was not at all sure why he had said it.

He frowned, remembering that in his second year of college, the only year he had been on the varsity team, he had proved an indifferent player.

"Not now," he whispered. "Not anymore."

He squashed the shape out of his beer can and stood it on top of the television.

THERE WAS A THUMP OVER HIS HEAD. THE CEILING creaked.

"Someone came home while I was in the shower," he said to himself, and ran his hand over his belly, feeling for signs of bloat from the beer.

He took the stairs in three leaps, strode into the master bedroom, calling, "Sherry?"

The dark figure in the room surprised Coach.

He yelled, "Hey!"

Daphne was dancing in front of the full-length mirror. She had improvised a look—sweeping her hair over her right ear, and stretching the neck of her shirt until her right shoulder was bared. A thing by the Commodores shrieked from her transistor.

"Nothing," she said.

"You're not home. Aren't you with whoosis? You're supposed to be out. You are *beet* red," Coach said.

Daphne lowered her head and squared her shirt, which bagged around her small torso. "Okay, Dad," she said.

"No, but how did your audience like the show? I bet they

loved it," Coach said. He smiled at himself in the mirror. "I'm just kidding you, Daph. You looked great."

"Come *on,* Dad," she said, and tried to pass.

Coach chimed in with the radio. He shuffled his feet. "Hey, Daph, you know what time it is?" he said.

"Let me out, please," Daphne said.

"It's monkey time!" Coach did a jerky turn, keeping in the way of the exit door. "Do the shing-a-ling. Do the Daphne." He rolled his shoulder vampishly. He kissed his own hand. He sang along.

"Thanks a lot," Daphne said. She gave up on trying to get around him. She leaned over and snapped off her radio. "You've got to use a mirror so you don't look stupid," she said. "Everybody does."

"I was only kidding. Seriously. I know dancing is important," Coach said.

"May I go now? I've got algebra." Daphne brought her hair from behind her ear.

"Before that, you have to hear the news. Here's a news bulletin, flash extra."

"You're drunk. You and Mom are going to live in different cities," Daphne said. "Somebody shot somebody."

"No, this is good news. I'm going to be coach here of the varsity. Me." Coach pointed to his chest.

"Now let me out, please," Daphne said.

Coach let her pass. He followed her down the narrow hallway to her bedroom.

"More money," he said. "I'll even be on TV. I'll have my own show on Sundays. And I'll get written up in the press all the time. By *real* reporters. Hey! Why am I yelling at wood, here?"

8

COACH WAS DRUNK AT THE KITCHEN TABLE. HE WAS enjoying the largeness of the room, and he was making out a roster for his dream team. He had put the best kids from his fifteen years of coaching in the positions they had played for him. He was puzzling over the tight-end spot. "Jim Wyckoff or Jerry Kinney?" he said aloud. He penciled "Kinney" into his diagram.

He heard Daphne on the stairs. It occurred to him to clear the beer cans from the table. Instead, he snapped open a fresh can. "Daphne?" he called.

"Wait a second. What?" she said from the living room.

"Just wondered who else was alive besides me," Coach said. "Your mom's still not home."

Daphne entered the kitchen.

"You're sorry you were rude before? That's perfectly okay, honey, just forget it. All right, Father, but I really am ashamed of myself anyway," Coach said.

"You guzzled all those?" Daphne said.

"Hold still. What've you got on?" Coach asked her. He hauled his chair around so that he could see his daughter.

"Two, four, five," Daphne said, counting the cans.

She was wearing one of the fan shirts that Coach had seen on a few summer coeds. On the front, against a maroon field, in gold, was GO. Across the back was GRIFFINS.

"Now you're talking," Coach said.

"It was free. This guy I met—well, these two guys, really—who work at Campus World, they gave it to me. It's dumb, but I want you to see I care. I do care. Not just for you, but because I want to stay here. Do you think we can maybe? Do your people look any good this year?"

"Winners," Coach said.

"Yeah," Daphne said.

Coach skidded his chair forward. "Have a beer," he said. "Sit down here and let me show you on paper the material they've given me to work with. Then maybe you'll be a believer. Now these guys are fast and big for once. I'm not overestimating them, either. I've seen what I've seen," Coach said.

A car crept into the drive, and then its engine noise filled the garage. Coach and Daphne were quiet until Sherry bustled down the short hall that connected the garage to the kitchen.

"Really late. Sorry, sorry," she said.

"It's a party in here, I warn you," Coach said.

"So I noticed." Sherry had a grocery sack, but it was almost empty. There were bright streaks of paint on her brown arms.

Daphne plucked a bag of Oreo cookies from the groceries.

"Shoot me one of those," Coach said.

"Is there any beer left for me?" Sherry said. "I want to drown my disappointment. I can't paint!"

"You *can* paint," Coach said.

"Let's face it," Sherry said. "An artist? The wife of a coach?"

You Know Charles

ALLEN WAS DRIVING HIS FATHER'S DODGE UP LIGHT Street, looking for an empty parking space near Cheshire Towers—the old Baltimore hotel turned apartment building. As he got close, Allen noticed an odd-faced teenager sitting on the steps of the Cheshire. The boy wore shorts and a cowboy hat. He was seated in the bleak sun, up from the shadows of the mighty shrubs that flanked the Cheshire's entrance.

Allen began breathing through his teeth. People like the teenager made Allen anxious.

The teenager bounced from his seat, and threw open the Cheshire's doors for a nurse in pale hose and crisp uniform. Allen pointed his father's car into the far-left lane of the street and kept on driving.

Allen's paternal aunt, Mindy, had a rental suite on the eleventh floor of the Cheshire Towers—a creamy, stone building, distinguishable for its many windows and the various drape styles and colors in them. Allen had left his home in Towson that morning on an impulse. He had felt the urge to chat his problems out with someone more mature.

"Aagh," he said, and stamped on the brakes for his fourth stoplight. "I hate this damn town. I really do! Row houses, shmow houses. Couldn't they think of something else?"

His generator light blinked on. With a little jump and an intake of breath, Allen saw the light and snapped off the air conditioner.

He found a parking slot in front of a necktie shop in an alley. The shop was open for Saturday business, but empty, except for a stout saleswoman who was planted, angrily, in the doorway.

"Bless you," Allen told the parking meter as he read its orders. He drew a shade with his hand over his eyebrows, and squinted at the façades of his aunt's apartment building. "Please, please be home," he said to the upper-floor windows when he found them. Allen adjusted his right foot in its penny loafer, and walked.

THE TEENAGER IN THE COWBOY HAT HAD COME OUT onto the broad sidewalk, and was watching as Allen approached.

Allen stalled, and got his bearings under a lilac bush. He busied himself with his wristwatch, shaking it and scowling at its face. It was eleven-forty.

"Guess how much I used to weigh," the teenager said. He held open the vest he wore instead of a shirt, and showed Allen his tiny waist and rib cage.

"You're crazy," Allen said.

"Yeah, but just guess," the boy said.

"Four hundred and fifty pounds," Allen said. He headed up the sidewalk, toward the entrance to the Cheshire.

The cowboy followed close on Allen's heels.

"You belong back in your room at the mental asylum," Allen said.

The cowboy took his hat, waved it with his hand, and did a low bow. "Monsieur."

Allen looked at the bent-over boy, saw the zodiac pendant hanging from his neck, the archless sandals of stitched plastic.

"You look about the right weight," Allen said, and swallowed.

"That's what I think," the cowboy said. He straightened up and took a soldierly stance. "It took willpower."

MINDY WAS PROPPED ON HER COUCH, ON FOAM PIL-lows the colors of Easter candy. She had a crocheted afghan spun twice around the calves of her legs.

The old suite she rented had been restyled with lowered ceilings and a pink-beige carpet. There was a new, folding door on the bathroom, and a line of little appliances in the kitchen.

The room seemed hushed after the street racket below, and the floor and furniture were striped with light that came through the window blind. Low on a wall, an air cooler was chugging.

"Ooh, thank heavens, you're here," Allen said. "Do you have any idea what would have happened to me if you'd been gone out to lunch or something?" He flopped down on the floor in front of Mindy, gripped the back of his neck, and let his head roll. "Whew, I'll tell you. I'd be at the police station right now, filling out reports. That's a tricky downtown, on a good day. But on a day like today—a Saturday, when everything's thronged—the people get irritable enough to kill one another, and they don't even know why. It's because they're hot."

Mindy was watching Allen without interest.

"Aunt Min, I hope you can help me," he said. "I need desperately for somebody to talk me out of doing something stupid."

Mindy creased the pages of the newspaper she had been reading and tossed them over her shoulder onto the floor behind the couch. She reached for a glass on the lamp table—a brown drink with a bobbing cherry.

"Give me a minute to get my equilibrium," Allen said. "Then I'll unload the whole problem. Your place sure is coming along. It looks better and better every time I come. Is that a new painting?"

Mindy lifted herself and craned her neck to see the wall behind her. "No," she said. She relaxed back into place, and tapped the cherry that floated on the surface of her drink. "I got that at an estate sale almost a year ago."

"What does it remind me of?" Allen said, thinking. "My head is full of names. I've been taking a course on the history of art—which I love. I was smart, for once, and got the jump on my graduating class. They don't start college until fall quarter. Rousseau is the name that keeps sticking in my mind for some reason—in relation to that one." He nodded at the wall. "Someone, either the textbook or my t.a., says the whole pageant of art history stops right with Henri Rousseau. I think I already knew that—but, anyway, his work sort of reminds you of looking through a magnifying glass. He can take you out into a field or a jungle, say, and leave you standing there. Painting, I found out, is all done with the eyes." Allen straightened his posture and pulled his feet into a lotus position.

"To prove what I mean, we saw these amazing films, of Jean Renoir, in his last and final days, where he was painting with brushes strapped to the backs of his wrists—which were crippled up with something, but even that didn't stop Renoir. Okay, you're not interested," Allen said. "But what brought all this up is I really do like your picture, if nothing else, just for the winter theme. I love winter, and I hate summer. You wouldn't believe how lazy I am because of the humidity recently. I just drop when it gets too bad, and Dad leaves our air conditioner off overnight, so you wake up already sick. One morning I was fixing cinnamon toast or something, and I had to practically lie on the counter to keep from going into a complete faint."

"How is Paul?" Mindy said.

"Fine," Allen said. "So what I do is throw a whole tray of ice cubes into the bathtub with me, first thing, and then I just stay there until the air conditioner's working enough to make some difference. I know it's not good for you, to go from red hot to freezing cold—it's probably why I'm so hoarse. Dad says I go around coughing twenty hours a day."

"Is Paul still thinking of remarrying?" Mindy said. She untangled her legs from the afghan, stood, and circled where Allen was positioned on the rug.

"That's the whole thing I came to talk to you about, Aunt Min." Allen looked up, and turned slowly on his seat, following Mindy. "The woman, it turns out—I've never met her. I just heard about her from Dad, and, of course, he left out all the bad stuff. She's older than he is. She's been married before, at least once. She's got four kids, which are grown, thank

God. He wants to move her—Laura Glinnis is, I guess, her name—into the house with us. You can imagine what that'd do to me. I've never had to live with a woman. Not since we lost Mom."

"You never lived with your mother, Allen. She died in childbirth."

"I know," Allen said, looking sad for a moment. "See, Dad's forgot all about Mom, that's what gets me." Allen pulled a burr from his sock and threw it onto the carpet. "I had the Dodge out one night, driving around, and thinking over this whole thing. I got off the beltway at some exit, and went to a bar and had a couple of mixed drinks. No one even asked for an i.d. They just served me the drinks, one on top of another. I was completely exhausted by then. I didn't care if Dad moved Mrs. Glinnis and her brood right smack into the dining room and fed them T-bone steaks. I started smashing my fist on the tabletop of the booth they had there. I didn't hurt anything really. Just my own hand. But I realized I have a capacity to be very destructive. It's like there's some monster inside me that wants to kill everything in my way."

"Why don't *you* get married, Allen?" Mindy said. She was between him and the couch, snapping at her manicured fingernails with her thumb. "Why don't you get a wife somewhere, and marry her, and move away?"

"I don't have anyone to marry," Allen said.

"I know dozens of people."

"That'd marry me?"

"In a minute," Mindy said.

"Yeah, okay. Only, so many people make me nervous. There was a kid out front today, for example."

"Tex? Tex is usually out front. You'd delight in him, Allen. He's got just the right touch of—"

"No, you must be thinking of someone else," Allen said.

MINDY WAS IN A BEAN-BAG CHAIR IN THE CORNER, loading film into her camera. "You know, I bought this camera with money I won in the football pools," she said. "I always win. That's why I love to gamble."

"What?" Allen said.

"Nothing," Mindy said. "Don't worry." Her chignon had come undone, and the left side of her hair—blonde, though she was fifty-one—had fallen onto the shoulder of her kimono. "I clicked off a couple I didn't mean to. It'll be all right."

"It will," Allen said, in a low voice to the cowboy-hatted teenager who sat on the couch with him. "She's really more or less a professional. Her work's appeared in a couple of the D.C. galleries—places you'd recognize if I could remember the names."

"One gallery. They just showed two of my self-portraits," Mindy said. "A picture of me at the stove, and one of me petting Abra."

"Cat that ran away," Allen told the cowboy.

Both young men had been drinking earnestly. Allen tugged off his cotton shirt and laid it out on the floor. He removed his loafers and his wristwatch. The cowboy took off his vest.

"What may I call you?" Allen asked.

The cowboy puffed his right cheek full of air, then noisily let the air out. "Baker," he said.

"First, or last?" Allen said.

The cowboy shrugged.

"Baker, alone, is fine," Allen said. "Easier to remember."

"One more minute," Mindy said from the corner. "I'm truly sorry this is taking so long. It isn't my fault. The spool's in backwards or something. I wouldn't have had Allen get you up here," she said to the cowboy, "if I'd known this was going to happen."

"These'll be great photographs," Allen said.

"Oops," Mindy said. "Oh, I did something, and now I can't—do you know anything about cameras?"

"I had a basic film theory and technique course," Allen said.

"Loading," Mindy said. "L-o-a-d-i-n-g."

"Not for *any* camera," Allen said.

Mindy struggled out of the bean-bag chair. She came toward them, stepping over the coffee table and showing one of her legs from the thigh down. She dropped the camera. Its timer ticked off fifteen seconds against the floor carpet.

Allen squeezed his forehead and sighed.

"The joke is, I do make good photographs," she said. "Maybe—who's to say?—great ones. But you've got to do daily work to be great, and for that you need a darkroom in your house, and not way across the g.d. town." She sat on the coffee table with her skirt hitched up.

"That's true," Allen said.

"I had a camera," Baker said.

"Good for you, Tex," Mindy said. "Seriously, I got two rolls of thirty-six people each. What did I just say? Did I say, 'thirty-six people each'? Isn't that a scream? Thirty-six *exposures* each."

"Faces?" Allen said.

"Yes, honey, that's what the world is. There's no world without faces. Look at that face."

Allen and Mindy looked at Baker.

He was whistling through a cavity in a front tooth. He wiggled his eyebrows at them, hard enough to make the brim of his cowboy hat move up and down.

"What's in that face, Allen?" Mindy said.

Allen narrowed his eyes at Baker, and asked him to turn his head left, then right.

"Well?" Mindy said.

"Well, because of the hat, he looks—I'd say Western."

"You're a sharp boy," Mindy said.

"I wasn't done," Allen said. "It also looks like a face that's recently lost weight."

"Yeah, I did," Baker said.

"You don't see any pain in those eyes?" Mindy asked Allen.

"Yes. Well, really, no. Frankly, I don't, Aunt Min, I don't."

"Good, because I don't, either. There isn't any. How about fear? Do you see fear in his eyes? Never mind." Mindy got up and headed for the bathroom.

"Do you like it hot, like this?" Allen asked Baker.

Baker looked around his feet, and then around the apartment.

"I mean, do you like hot weather?"

"Sure," Baker said.

Mindy came back and Allen stood up. Baker gathered his vest, and stood up as well.

"Here's a face. Sit down, both of you," she said. She showed them a photograph of a young fellow whose head was shaved and whose eyes were wild-looking. There were markings, or scratches, on the photo, above the dark eyes. "This one is disturbed. People call him disturbed. But he made perfect sense to me the day I took pictures of him. It's one reason I wanted to photograph you two," Mindy said.

"Not that you're retarded," Allen said to Baker. "Or me— that I am."

"Oh, you're retarded, all right," Mindy said. "I don't know how, Allen, but you got all stunted up at the age of six."

"Hey, that's the bottle talking," Allen said.

"This was nice," the cowboy said to Mindy. "I'd like to visit you again sometime in the future."

"Good, Tex. When?" Mindy said.

MINDY HAD FELT SICK, GRABBED UP ALLEN'S SHIRT, and gone swiftly into the bathroom with the shirt held against her mouth. For a long while, Allen heard faucet water running. Eventually, he tried pushing open the folding door.

"Aunt Min?"

The door moved a few inches, and caught on Mindy, who lay over the floor tiles with Allen's shirt balled under her cheek for a pillow.

Allen pulled the door shut. He paced around the apartment in just his slacks, hissing and swearing to himself. He perched on the back of Mindy's couch, and brought the telephone to his lap. He dialed "1" and then his home phone number.

"Hello," said a woman's voice, startling Allen.

"Is this my house?" he said. "Who is this?"

"I'm Laura Glinnis," the woman said.

"Well, put Dad on if he's there. I need to talk with him immediately."

"Just a second, Allen," Mrs. Glinnis said. "Paul?"

"What do you want?" Allen's father said into the phone.

"Just to let you know what I'm up to," Allen said.

"Is it serious?"

"I feel that this time I'm in deep water, Dad. Things are completely out of my control. I'm sauced, for one thing. There might even be an ambulance case in the bathroom. I'm so messed up," Allen said.

There was a long silence at the other end of the line.

Allen heard the whispery-scrape of a cupped palm over the phone's mouthpiece. His father's voice came back, slowly saying, "Relax, boy. Run this thing down for me, step by step."

"Okay," Allen said. "Now the first thing you should know is I came here to tell Aunt Mindy about what's been happening—my side of the story."

"Who's in the bathroom hurt?" Allen's father said. "Is it Mindy? Tell me straight. Take it slow now, son."

"Aunt Mindy'll be fine. I'm not worried about her," Allen said. "She's used to being drunk."

"Allen?" the voice said. "Do you know how you make me feel?"

"Yeah, yeah," Allen said, and smacked down the phone's receiver.

HE STRAIGHTENED THE APARTMENT A LITTLE, TI-died the kitchen, and perked coffee. He opened the bathroom door the few inches it would go. He hoped the coffee aroma would revive Mindy.

"You know Charles," Mindy said in her sleep.

Allen got the camera off the floor, and sat down, and tried until he was sweating to get the roll of film untangled.

"I feel so regretful!" Mindy called.

Allen looked in on her. She was awake, but in the same prone position. Water still splashed from the opened faucet.

"This is disgusting, I know," she said. "It must be disgusting for you to see, Allen. A young boy. I'm really so, so sorry."

"You're forgiven," Allen said.

"Do you mean it? You're not really angry?"

"Hell, no. Not at all," Allen said.

Whistling to himself, he borrowed a tailored shirt from a hanger in Mindy's closet. He rolled the cuffs, where there were flower-shaped pearl buttons. He turned the collar under, uncomfortably.

In the kitchen, Allen poured coffee into one of his aunt's pretty teacups. He sat in the tiny dining annex, his legs crossed. He sipped coffee and considered his day. He thought he'd drive out around the Baltimore zoo—maybe buy himself some dinner.

I Am Twenty-One

I HEARD RINGING, AND I REALIZED THAT WHAT I
had done was continued my answer to Essay Question I—"What
effect did the discovery of the barrel vault have on the archi-
tecture of 13th century cathedrals?"—writing clockwise in the
left, top, and right-hand margins of page one in my exam book.
I had forgotten to move along to page two or to Essay Question II. The ringing was coming from in me—probably from
overdoing it with diet pills or from the green tea all last night
and from reading so much all the time.

I was doing C work in all courses but this one—"The
Transition from Romanesque to Gothic." I needed to blast this
course on its butt, and that was possible because for this course
I knew it all. I needed only time and space to tell it. My study
notes were 253 pencil sketches from slides we had seen and from
plates in books at the Fine Arts Library and some were from our
text. I had sixty-seven pages of lecture notes that I had copied
over once for clarity. Everything Professor Williamson had said

in class was recorded in my notes—practically even his throat clearings and asides about the weather. It got to the point where if he rambled, I thought, yeah, yeah, cut the commercial and get back to the program.

Some guy whose hair I could've ripped out was finished with his exam. He was actually handing it to the teaching assistant. How could he be *finished,* have given even a cursory treatment to the three questions? He was a quitter, a skimmer, I decided; a person who knew shit about detail.

I was having to stop now and then, really too often, to skin the tip of my pencil with the razor blade I had brought along. I preferred a pencil because it couldn't dry up or leak. But this was a Number 2 graphite and gushy-gummy and I was writing the thing away. The eraser was just a blackened nub. Why hadn't I brought a damn *box* of pencils?

The teaching assistant was Clark—Clark Something or Something Clark, I didn't know. He was baggy and sloppy, but happy-looking. He had asked me out once for Cokes, but I had brushed him off. That was maybe stupid because he might've been in charge of grading exams.

I decided to ignore Essay Question II, pretend I hadn't even seen it. I leaned hard into Question III, on church decoration, windows, friezes, flora, fauna, bestiaries, the iconography in general. I was quoting Honorius of Autun when the class bell fired off.

I looked up. Most people were gone.

"Come on, everyone!" Clark called. "Please. Come on now. Miss Bittle? Mr. Kenner, please. Miss Powers?"

"Go blow, Clark," I said right out loud. But I slapped him

my exam booklet and hurried out of Meverett, feeling let down and apathetic all of a sudden, and my skin going rubbery cold.

I BIKED HOME WITH A LOT OF TROUBLE. I WENT ON the sidewalks. I was scared that in the streets I'd get my ringing confused with car warnings.

I was still ringing.

Last semester I had had a decorating idea for my apartment, this monastic idea of strict and sparse. I had stripped the room down to a cot, a book table, one picture. The plaster walls were a nothing oatmeal color, which was okay. But not okay was that some earlier renter had gooped orange—unbelievably—paint on the moldings and window frames. So where I lived looked not like a scholar's den, finally, but more like a bum's sleepover, like poverty.

My one picture up wasn't of a Blessed Virgin or a detail from Amiens of the King of Judah holding a rod of the Tree of Jesse. Instead, it was an eight-by-ten glossy of Rudy and Leslie, my folks. Under the backing was written *Gold Coast, the first cool day.* The photo had been shot out on North Lake Shore Drive around 1964, I'd say, when I was three. Leslie, my mom, was huddled into Rudy, sharing his lined leather jacket. They appeared, for all the eye sparkle, like people in an engagement-ring ad. I kept the picture around because, oddly, putting away the *idea* of my folks would've been worse than losing the real them. In the photo, they at least *looked* familiar.

They had been secret artists. Rudy was a contractor for a living, Leslie a physical therapist. So they worked all their art urges out on me—on my school projects, for instance, which they hurled themselves into. One project "I did" for seventh grade that they helped me with was, I swear, good enough for a world's fair. It was a kind of three-dimensional diorama triptych of San Francisco Bay with both bridges—Oakland and Golden Gate—that may have even lit up or glowed in the dark. We had to borrow a neighbor's station wagon just to get the thing safely over to Dreiser Junior High—it lined up as long as an ironing board.

I GOT MY BIKE TUGGED INSIDE, LEFT IT LEANING against the wall under the photograph. I clapped a kettle onto the midget stove in my kitchen part of the apartment, and paced, waiting for the water to heat. The pitch of the steam when it got going was only a quarter tone below the ringing in my head.

My folks were two and a half years gone.

I used to drive out to the site of their accident all the time—a willow tree on Route 987. The last time I went, the tree was still healing. The farmlands were a grim powdery blond in the white sun, and the earth was still ragged from winter. I sat there in my tiny Vega on the broken crumbly shoulder. The great tree and the land around—flat as a griddle for miles and miles—didn't seem as fitting as I had once thought, not such a poetic place for two good lives to have stopped.

I had my tea now and grieved about the exam. Leaving a whole essay question unanswered! How could I expect to get better than a C?

Just before my first sip of tea, my ringing shut off as though somebody had punched a button, said, "Enough of that for her."

I decided it was time to try for sleep, but first I used a pen with a nylon point to tattoo a P on the back of my hand. This meant when I woke up I was to eat some protein—shrimp or eggs or a green something.

On the cot I tried, as a sleep trick, to remember my answer to Essay Question I—word for fucking word.

Smart

MOM SENT MY BROTHER, JACKIE, OVER FROM WHEEL-ing to take care of me the last week of March, right before I had the baby. I was living in D.C., alone, in five rooms of a sagging apartment house called The Augusta, on Wisconsin Avenue, opposite the National Cathedral. The Augusta was a worn, white building, and it shone behind me, cold and crooked in the sun of a false spring. I was waiting on the sidewalk for Jackie's car. Across the wide dangerous street, the cathedral's huge towers and many points glowered. I had been waiting for over two hours, which was the longest I'd been out of my rooms for months, including trips two blocks away to see my O.B.

I was living mostly in the study then. It was a dim room that smelled of old drapes and waxed paneling and rusty radiator heat. I spent my hours there in a resident chair that was covered with some kind of bristly horsehair, like an old theater seat. The chair had a cracked foot and leaned, perforce, into a corner. One nice thing in the room, some people would think, was a little window with diamond panes of blue and brown glass.

When I got up from the chair, it was just to change a record, or twist my spine, or to nibble some of the food my neighbor, Mrs. Sally Dixon, brought me. Mrs. Dixon was eighteen years old; terribly shy. She always said, "This is Mrs. Dixon" when she knocked on the door, so I never called her Sally. I liked that she didn't try to talk with me when she came—twice a week or so, all winter—to stock my cramped kitchen with cans and boxes. Before her visits, I always spent a lot of time on my appearance so she wouldn't worry about the baby. Still, I could see her distress whenever she actually *faced* me, to accept my grocery lists, or my money, or my thanks.

I wore socks usually, but no shoes, and, always—because it was the only covering that still fitted me—a cottony slip that had been my mom's: blue, size sixteen. I normally had some sweaters on over the slip. I had one expensive lamb's-wool cardigan. My hair was wrecked by pregnancy. It swelled in a cloud around my small face.

WHEN JACKIE ARRIVED, HE SURPRISED ME BY BEING a pedestrian—by stepping out from behind a cluster of tourists on their way to the big church. I had expected him to drive up, in his West Virginia car.

He gave me an impatient kiss and began scolding. "Aw, don't tell me. You can't be on the level. You couldn't have stood outside here, waiting since four o'clock."

"I didn't know if you could find my place," I said.

"Hell, I *found* it forty minutes ago. But they don't want you to park your car in this city. I've been going up one way and down the other. Finally, I just got out, set the car loose, and told it, 'Every man for himself.' Is this your place here? Looks pretty good. You don't look very good."

He frowned as if I shouldn't have been in my own body.

I led him inside, and he gave me more of the same. He took one look at the ratty magazines, the plates and glasses in unhealthy stacks, the empty jar of Nescafé, the slumping rows of record albums. He said, "I'm sorry, Eleanor, but I'm mad."

He stalked out the apartment door. I followed him down through the little lobby, with its tiled floor and round mirrors, to The Augusta's front walkway. The sun had dimmed, and the temperature had dropped about ten degrees.

Jackie scuffed his shoes on the cement awhile, and then he went into a shallow park that was between The Augusta and her taller, newer neighbor, The Frontenac. He tapped a few trees. He had a cigarette.

"That's the scariest damn church I've ever seen!" he called to me.

"It's the National," I said.

"I know it. Of course. I'm going for my luggage, Eleanor, and then I want to start straightening up that mess in there. Are you going to stand around on the sidewalk, pregnant?"

"I've got to be here in order to let you in," I said. "The front door locks itself once I go through."

WHEN HE GOT A FEW PIECES OF HIS LUGGAGE SAFELY inside, some of the irritation went out of him. He put me in my chair, and gave me the cap from the thermos he had used on his road trip. The cap was full of still-warm cocoa that Mom, back home, had made for us.

"Really," Jackie said, as he pushed around the furniture. He yanked the vacuum cleaner from the closet, and bullied it over the rugs in the study and hall and in the old living room, which I had fixed up for the baby. I opened a Modern Library edition of *Cousin Bette* and pretended to read it.

Jackie was in and out for the next few hours, until after dark. He reported to me every so often. "All right. There's a good hardware just two blocks from here, and now we've got decent light bulbs, at least, and some emergency candles.

"Get me up at eight o'clock tomorrow morning, Eleanor. I have to move my car from across the street, or I'll never move it again, because the police'll put a boot on it.

"You do have an alarm clock? Because we'll need it, and if you don't, the hardware store's open until six.

"There's a good pharmacy close. Closes at ten."

I heard him dragging open drawers, loading things into closets. "One more haul from the car," he said.

About nine that evening, he made his last trip in, with a purplish leather shaving kit that had been our father's, and, under his left arm, a cardboard six-pack of drinking glasses. "Look here. They were selling these at that grocery for three bucks," he said. "Tumblers."

When everything was put away, we went to inspect the room I had arranged for the baby. It was a green and yellow place, though I was banking on a girl. There were two pieces of Bambi furniture, and gowns and outfits still in gift boxes, and Fisher Price toys some relatives had sent. I had hung up an Animaland poster, and strung a fruit and flowers mobile over the crib. On the floor, there was a fierce, icy-looking polish that Jackie had produced with mop and wax.

"Tonight, I'm going to sleep like the dead," he said.

"Me, too. I've had it," I said.

I went to the dining room—a windowless nook at one end of the kitchen. I had had the movers wedge my tall bed into this area. It had been a lifelong habit of mine to sleep near the center of activity in a house. I wouldn't have felt safe in the back bedroom.

I was thirty-six—old for a first baby, I know. In nine months, I had gained forty pounds, and I'd been trying to cut back in the last weeks. I had a dream that first night Jackie was there. Apples, pears, and squash rolled by. I saw a table laid with a roast, glazed carrots, salty potatoes. A voice told me, "Eleanor! Eat these."

Jackie was up, drinking coffee and scrambling eggs, in what seemed to be the middle of the night. I lay on my back, in bed, in a little bit of pain. I watched him, framed by the kitchen portal, as he hunted for utensils, checked plates and glasses for stains, and chatted out loud. Every few minutes his panicky activity would stop, and he would stand and seem to dissolve into himself.

"I forgot what I was going to say," he whispered.

"What?" I said.

"Do you want to wake up? It's seven-thirty. I've got to go move my car. Oh, don't tell me it's raining."

"Probably. It's been so nice. We had weather in the high sixties. On one day, we—"

"Before you go on, I want to tell you this." Jackie had some coffee and then stepped out of the kitchen and sat at the foot of my bed. "When it's time for us to go, and you're ready for the baby, you should already have packed your nightwear, and so forth. You know—toothbrush, robe, slippers. Stay awake, Eleanor. I want to tell you this, and then I've got to get my car moved."

"Okay, I'm listening," I said. "I think today I'd like to sit on a bench outside and watch the rain."

"Smart," Jackie said.

I rose, yawning and stretching, and waddled to the record player. "I wish you'd have let me sleep," I said. "I haven't had *dream* sleep in about four weeks. The place looks nice, Jackie. Thank you a lot for cleaning."

"What do you want for breakfast? Tell me fast," he said. "Got to get sliding."

"Nothing," I said. I went to the shelf in the closet and got out a lap blanket.

"Well, if you don't eat, and you're not sleeping, you'll have a terrible baby. I'm here to make sure you take care of yourself."

"Look at me," I said, heading for my three-legged chair. "Could you lie down and sleep comfortably, do you think? Or eat? Imagine a big pointy rock turning in your stomach. Roaring up your throat."

"Hmph," Jackie said.

He was shaking his raincoat, getting ready to put it on.

JACKIE HAD HIS OWN DISAPPOINTMENTS. ON THE drive to D.C., he had got tar all over the flanks and bumpers of his new car. He had, he said, a mean sore throat. But his real depression came from the fact that he had somehow failed his comprehensive exams in clinical psychology at Marshall University. So, as a result, they weren't giving him his degree.

"Mom pressured me into coming here and nursemaiding you," he said. "She thought it was a way out for both of us."

We were in the study. Jackie was combing through *The Washington Post* for something to read. For Jackie, a newspaper had always meant more physical exercise than actual reading. He read standing, with the paper held high, and at his spread arms' length. He would rush through a section, his arms closing and opening, the paper beating like big wings. Whenever he paused, it was just long enough to cock his head and brood a few seconds over some column or picture, before his arms snapped again, and he moved ahead. He used the little intervals, when the paper was closed and his fingers were pinching off a new page, to raise his chin and stretch his neck—as if he were fighting a headache. He brushed through the financial section, discarded it, and started on the editorials.

"What's in there? Nothing?" I said.

"Nothing," he said.

THAT WAS TYPICAL OF JACKIE—AND OF ME. WE weren't learners, really. We had spent our lives rushing through everything: music albums, books—though never a *whole* book from start to finish. We took in whatever we thought we could turn into conversation, from TV shows, movies. The only reason we liked to know a thing was so we'd have something to yammer about—not that we had anyone to share our talk with.

"Let's get a breath," Jackie said. "Can you walk? The walls are closing in on me."

We walked toward downtown. There was still some orange-ish sun on the buildings, but the stores and cars were burning lights. In a chained-off, empty parking lot, beside a closed gas station, some rangy black men were playing basketball. One man, bearded and in a wool cap, dodged around two defenders and sprang and fired a shot at the brick wall of the gas station.

"They don't have a basket," Jackie said. "There's your metaphor for urban blight."

"This isn't really the blighted part of town," I said. "Those guys are probably ambassadors from the Zimbabwe Embassy."

"Probably," Jackie said, but he looked a little surprised. "Can I ask you something?"

"Normally when people ask if they can ask, I say no. But go ahead," I said.

"Well, Eleanor, what do you intend to do?"

I tapped my stomach. "When this is over, I'm going to crash-diet, drink real tea for a change, and I thought I'd hunt up a filing job, or maybe be a salesgirl at Saks."

"The point is, it's not going to be over," Jackie said. "Not at the hospital. Not for at least twenty years is this going to be over, and that's if you get most of the breaks. It makes my head swim. It'll probably *never* be over."

"Tell me something new," I said.

A jogger went by, hurdling some traffic cones, and started a couple of dogs barking. I was ready, right then, to have the baby. I wasn't sure of the date, and didn't want to be. I might have been overdue. The one night with Phil had been in early June.

"You're going to run very quickly through the rest of Dad's money, especially in this rook-joint city. I was just wondering how you plan to live? It's supposed to cost something like nine hundred thousand *dollars* to raise a kid these days."

"What do you want me to do?" I said.

"Not you," Jackie said. "Phil! Doesn't Phil ever say anything?"

"All the time," I said. "He says he'll do everything a human being can possibly do."

Jackie hissed and gestured at the buildings around us with both arms. "Oh, Eleanor, *think!*" he said. "Where *is* he?"

PHIL WAS ELEVEN YEARS YOUNGER THAN I, AND WE'D been engaged to be married, had lived together for a long time before I broke things off. But we never were very close. Phil carried our courtship and cohabitation as he carried most every situation—with a lot of bluster and bluff. He had a broad, heavy accent that, for all I know, was faked. He said his sentences had "reverse spin." He was incapable of talking to people, it seemed, without moving toward them and actually taking them in his hands, or roping an arm over their shoulders, or, at least, resting a finger on their lapels. Constantly, and toward no end that I could see, he *lied*. If asked where he was from, he would say, "Originally? Pensacola," or, "*All* over. I'm an Army brat."

The one last time, in early June, happened after a pool party in Woodbury Hills, in Wheeling. I hadn't seen Phil for months, but I asked him to drive me to West Virginia for my mom's birthday. He was entertaining enough on the long nervous trip across Maryland and Pennsylvania. He told me a lot of—I'm sure—*lies* about his tour of duty in Vietnam, to keep my mind off the big hills and the sixteen-wheelers that blew around us. At a rest stop in New Stanton he bought me a souvenir paper booklet about Amish cooking. He had raised a dark beard, which worked a wonder for his face, giving him a strong, sharp chin where he had had none, and setting off his black eyes.

The pool party we went to was given by the Zigglers: twins, who were classmates of Jackie's at Marshall U. They were beautiful lean girls, each with a fat brown braid that went between her shoulders. On the party day, their tan skin was oiled, and they wore matching orange bandeau bikinis and pearl earbobs.

I never removed the long blue football jersey I was wearing, but sunned my legs from a lounger, and watched Phil doing laps in the pool. His arms pointed in easy arcs, and his legs pounded the water without throwing up much splash.

He sat with me for a moment as he toweled off his hair and beard. He called to Jackie, "Hey, champ! Going to get yourself wet today?"

Jackie hadn't even brought a swimsuit. He was down on the Zigglers' lawn, where he had cornered a Collie dog. He seemed to be holding the dog back with both arms, talking intently to it while he ruffled its ears and scratched the back of its neck.

Brenda Ziggler joined us. She looked pleasantly harassed by her hostess duties. She was streaming water, and there were wet highlights left on her torso and nice legs.

"Here's a guy who looks capable of building a grill fire for us," she said to Phil.

"Hey, I'm a *guest*," he said.

"Well, we can all just go hungry, I guess," Brenda said.

"I don't know where anything *is*," Phil said as he stroked his beard.

"Follow me," Brenda said, and Phil went along.

He was still excited, I could tell, on the ride back to my mom's house that evening. And though I knew that the glow he had, and the involuntary smile, were from being with the Zigglers and not me, just the same, he was something. I didn't even mind his built-up tennis shoes, or the silver saint on a chain around his neck.

In Mom's driveway, he sat on the hood of his car and spun his keys with one finger. When he spoke to me, I noticed a sweet grape Life Saver staining his tongue.

Jackie, who had been sullen in the back seat for the ride, went into the house alone. Phil and I decided to scare up a bar and get drunk.

I explained this whole episode to Jackie, a month or so later, over the phone.

"Fine," he said lifelessly.

"Okay. But it's a fact."

I heard him cough and clear his throat. "You don't *stay* pregnant at thirty-six," he said. He was in his typical bad mood, just off from interning at the County Mental Health Center. "A place," he once told me, "in what you might call a ghetto, uglier than any bowling alley, where they've never heard of air-conditioning."

He said how my baby could be born an idiot because of my age. "Not to mention who its father is," he said. He talked about postpartum depression and what it had done to our grandma.

I waited until he was through, and then I put down the telephone and went into my kitchen and kicked a utility pipe that was ticking there. When I came back, I said, "You can go to hell, Jackie. Let me speak to Mom."

PHIL APPEARED ONE EVENING, TWO DAYS BEFORE I went into labor. He had a small rocking chair and four card-board boxes—"cases," he called them—of baby food in the trunk of his car. He improvised and said he had been away for a while, in Chicago, helping some brother-in-law set up a construction firm.

I let him inspect the baby's room, and then we toured the rest of the place. It was the first time Phil had been inside The Augusta, and he told me, in a critical tone, that he approved. He spotted Jackie, who was on the floor by the TV, shelling peanuts and watching *Wonder Woman*.

"Say, champ," Phil said. "Or is it Doctor Champ now?"

Jackie snapped a peanut and swore. He looked hurt when he turned back to *Wonder Woman*, and after a bit he pulled himself off the floor and retreated to the kitchen.

We heard him running the electric mixer for the next twenty minutes, and then I detected a cake baking. I excused myself and peeked in on Jackie. He was up on the counter, furiously thrashing a wooden spoon around a bowl of cake frosting that was pressed between his thighs.

"Will you please be willing to *eat* some of this?" he said.

I went back to the study, where the TV was still on, its picture rolling and flashing. Phil had gone out to his car and brought in a gray metal box from which he emptied two checkbooks, a ledger tablet, a sawed-down pencil, and some stock certificates. He was in my three-legged chair.

"Let's see," I said, but he waved me off. He put the pencil lengthwise in his mouth, and shuffled his papers for a while before he spoke.

I stuck on an old record by Lambert, Hendricks, and Ross.

"Man, *good!*" Jackie yelled from the kitchen.

Phil said, "Turn it down, will you, princess?"

He pressed forward in the chair, but couldn't seem to get

started at what he wanted to say. He directed his small eyes at me and smiled without separating his lips. He beat his ledger tablet against his leg.

I said, "This is about the future, right?"

"Indeed," he said.

He began slowly, but then he got a little wound up. He talked about schools, coaches, music lessons—flute or piano? He was wondering aloud about a dental insurance plan when Jackie came in carrying a plate of cake and a coffee cup, which he had pushed against his stomach. He was watching the coffee, moving one step at a time. He got seated on the rug and looked at Phil, who had kept on talking, and was now nodding at Jackie.

Phil said, "A lot of my life, as you know, has been spent kicking around, spinning my tires, and going from job to job, which was great, because I learned a hell of a lot about *people*. I found out about people involved in war—sick people, some of them, and healthy . . ."

"Red-headed people and non-redheads," Jackie said.

Phil went on. "This business with my brother-in-law in Chicago, for example. That got me squared around and I did him a lot of good, though I won't see a damn lot of money from it. But I did see how you *make* money," he said. "You make money with people, princess. And people take to me. They like me. And if being liked isn't the whole war, it sure as hell is one big battle in the campaign."

"Boy, this is good for a mix," Jackie interrupted. He pointed at the cake with his flatware.

Phil kept going. His speech was rushed and urgent-sounding. "I haven't got a lot of what they call liquid assets," he said. "But I can read people like you two would read a book, and anything I'd want to get serious about, my people-reading talent would make me a success.

"I've got some things lined up for now and some for later," he said. "Step One, though, is a vet friend of mine who's in shipping and receiving for a big auto-parts warehouse and who's going to get me a job as a dispatcher, which I could easily handle. That position opens up in a month or two, when the guy they got now retires."

"In a month or two," Jackie said. He rose and changed the Lambert, Hendricks, and Ross record for a Duke Ellington. He put the needle down on "Cottontail," then sat again behind his coffee cup and plate.

Phil stopped talking and stared at Jackie and then at the record player. "Weird," Phil said. He sort of shook his head and then went on some more. "Step Two is an idea I've had for a long time and which I hope to activate through a contact of mine at the Coca-Cola headquarters in Atlanta, Georgia. It's so simple it's genius. Dietary Popsicles. You got diet soda, which sells like mad, and you got fat people who suffer more than anyone else in the heat and who could eat a million of these Popsicles to cool down, and never gain an ounce. And it *works.* I know, because I put Tab and Fresca in my ice-cube trays, and they freeze and they still taste good."

"I hope you don't *buy* any of this," Jackie said to me. He lifted his coffee cup, and its cork coaster stuck to the cup bottom.

"Naw, naw," I said.

"You don't?" Phil said, and looked puzzled.

Jackie and I waggled our heads in the negative.

"You say I lie?" Phil said.

"No, Phil," Jackie said.

I sucked a breath. "It's just that people, they don't ever do what they don't want to do. And they can't ever be what they aren't already."

Jackie said, "The biggest favor you could do this baby, and its mom, is just to realize that."

THE SAD THING WAS, IT HAD BEEN FUN LISTENING TO Phil. There was great authority in his delivery. For an instant there I had wanted to *be* him, or at least his age, and have his ideas.

Anyway, his manner became rather formal and unnaturally polite. He suddenly offered to leave because of the "weekend traffic."

"All right," Jackie and I said in unison.

Phil stood, put a hand on his head, and smoothed the hair there. I noticed for the first time that day that he had shaved off his beard. He was wearing his pointed boots, beltless slacks, and a canary-colored Ban-Lon shirt. I remembered that these were not clothes he got into on Saturdays, as my dad might have. They were the clothes Phil *wore*. He loaded up his utility box and put it under his arm, and then he shook hands with Jackie.

"Thank you for the baby presents," I said.

Phil said, "I'll be around, almost certainly, tomorrow, princess, with a lot more stuff."

"Don't worry," I said.

We heard his car gunning off. Phil had tuned the engine to make a lot of noise.

Jackie paced for a minute or two, and then he said, "Thank God, thank God!"

"What?" I said.

"Nothing."

"No, tell me."

"All right, I will," Jackie said. "Thank God you didn't make Phil part of the family."

"Halt," I said. "Phil is *very* important to me. When he goes on like that, I don't really mind."

"Eleanor," Jackie said, "he's a wrong number. Something small and slimy that you throw back. God, what he says about your self-concept."

"What does he say?"

"Nothing, except that you're very, very bad off. I can't explain it if you don't already know."

"The psychologist," I said.

"Yeah, well," Jackie said. He started pacing again.

"Look, I *know* I'm not smart," I said. "I don't particularly *want* to be smart. That's the whole difference between us—*I* don't torture myself by going around with people who are smart."

"That's right. That's terrific," Jackie said before I hurried out of the room.

From my high bed, I had a side-window view of a corner of the big cathedral. The church looked black and threatening, but very meaningful, to me. I decided I'd never move out of The Augusta. Phil would probably continue to come by for a while. Maybe Jackie would stay. Mrs. Dixon would come by, and eventually maybe she and I would have a nice conversation—or a meal together. Or not. There'd be another Mrs. Dixon, surely, if mine tired out. There'd be another Phil.

Yours

ALLISON STRUGGLED AWAY FROM HER WHITE RE-
nault, limping with the weight of the last of the pumpkins. She
found Clark in the twilight on the twig-and-leaf-littered porch
behind the house.

He wore a wool shawl. He was moving up and back in a
padded glider, pushed by the ball of his slippered foot.

Allison lowered a big pumpkin, let it rest on the wide floor
boards.

Clark was much older—seventy-eight to Allison's thirty-
five. They were married. They were both quite tall and looked
something alike in their facial features. Allison wore a natural-
hair wig. It was a thick blonde hood around her face. She was
dressed in bright-dyed denims today. She wore durable clothes,
usually, for she volunteered afternoons at a children's day-care
center.

She put one of the smaller pumpkins on Clark's long lap.
"Now, nothing surreal," she told him. "Carve just a *regular* face.
These are for kids."

In the foyer, on the Hepplewhite desk, Allison found the maid's chore list with its cross-offs, which included Clark's supper. Allison went quickly through the day's mail: a garish coupon packet, a bill from Jamestown Liquors, November's pay-TV program guide, and the worst thing, the funniest, an already opened, extremely unkind letter from Clark's relations up North. "You're an old fool," Allison read, and, "You're being cruelly deceived." There was a gift check for Clark enclosed, but it was uncashable, signed, as it was, "Jesus H. Christ."

LATE, LATE INTO THIS NIGHT, ALLISON AND CLARK gutted and carved the pumpkins together, at an old table set on the back porch, over newspaper after soggy newspaper, with paring knives and with spoons and with a Swiss Army knife Clark used for exact shaping of tooth and eye and nostril. Clark had been a doctor, an internist, but also a Sunday watercolorist. His four pumpkins were expressive and artful. Their carved features were suited to the sizes and shapes of the pumpkins. Two looked ferocious and jagged. One registered surprise. The last was serene and beaming.

Allison's four faces were less deftly drawn, with slits and areas of distortion. She had cut triangles for noses and eyes. The mouths she had made were just wedges—two turned up and two turned down.

By one in the morning they were finished. Clark, who had bent his long torso forward to work, moved back over to the glider and looked out sleepily at nothing. All the lights were out across the ravine.

Clark stayed. For the season and time, the Virginia night

was warm. Most leaves had been blown away already, and the trees stood unbothered. The moon was round above them.

Allison cleaned up the mess.

"Your jack-o'-lanterns are much, much better than mine," Clark said to her.

"Like hell," Allison said.

"Look at me," Clark said, and Allison did.

She was holding a squishy bundle of newspapers. The papers reeked sweetly with the smell of pumpkin guts.

"Yours are *far* better," he said.

"You're wrong. You'll see when they're lit," Allison said.

She went inside, came back with yellow vigil candles. It took her a while to get each candle settled, and then to line up the results in a row on the porch railing. She went along and lit each candle and fixed the pumpkin lids over the little flames.

"See?" she said.

They sat together a moment and looked at the orange faces.

"We're exhausted. It's good-night time," Allison said. "Don't blow out the candles. I'll put in new ones tomorrow."

THAT NIGHT, IN THEIR BEDROOM, A FEW WEEKS EARlier in her life than had been predicted, Allison began to die. "Don't look at me if my wig comes off," she told Clark. "Please."

Her pulse cords were fluttering under his fingers. She raised her knees and kicked away the comforter. She said something to Clark about the garage being locked.

At the telephone, Clark had a clear view out back and down to the porch. He wanted to get drunk with his wife once more. He wanted to tell her, from the greater perspective he had, that to own only a little talent, like his, was an awful, plaguing thing; that being only a little special meant you expected too much, most of the time, and liked yourself too little. He wanted to assure her that she had missed nothing.

He was speaking into the phone now. He watched the jack-o'-lanterns. The jack-o'-lanterns watched him.

Falling Away

"COME ON, VAN, CAN'T YOU REMEMBER?" I SAID.

"I'm trying, but no. An image here and there, the shirt I got blood on, the taste—frightening!" said Van to me, but really more to our marriage counselor, Shirley Salizar.

"You weren't wearing your glasses," I said. "Certainly weren't measuring your steps."

"All true," Van said.

Mrs. Salizar was letting the exchange play out. She looked drowsy this August early morning, a little dulled. Her eyes lately had been too much white in her tanned-up face, and there was today a burr caught on the hem of her navy sundress. Behind her, her fern plant had toppled and was spilling soil. She was forty-five, handsome if somewhat breastless. Petite.

I made small moans I hoped Shirley'd hear over the gurgle of the air conditioner. These were because Van was not explaining how a few nights before he had tripped on the kitchen landing, rumbled into our refrigerator, cracking his nose.

There was no desk in Shirley's office, just chairs. She was, as

usual, placed closer to Van than to me, and was roughly mim-
icking his sitting posture.

My secret low opinion of Shirley Salizar didn't matter to
me. I figured even a dolt could tell someone if he had something
like a hole in the back of his sweater and didn't know it.

So I kept talking into the rare chance for me to talk. I told
Shirley. She made not even the occasional glance to Van for ver-
ification. She glared at me as if I were a liar.

She liked to call Van's and my relationship "the patient."

Van was the patient.

And I minded her and Van's forming this little coalition
against me. Just to stay a *guest* at their discussions, I had had
to pretend I agreed I was "creator of the context" for what was
wrong with Van, for his big symptom, which was that he was
accident-prone. Very prone.

He had totaled our Nova, crashed on his bicycle, stumbled
on the porch stoop, and once chipped the bone in his chin. He
had dropped an outboard motor on his ankle—fractured the
ankle. He had caught fire at our stove, over the coals of the hi-
bachi, one time simply lighting his pipe.

"THIS LATEST SAVES YOU FROM HAVING TO HIT HIM
in the nose," Shirley said now. "Which may be the reason you've
kept him so clumsy."

My breath went out and I had trouble pulling in another.

"It is?" Van asked.

One chief reason we had chosen Shirley to help us with our
young marriage was that her office was in a skinny two-story on

the same lane as our house—very good for when we were out of a car or between cars.

"Enough," I said, finally. "Enough of the two against one, and of puzzling over possible motives, as if there's any *mystery* here."

Shirley's one first prescription, which she told us in our beginning session, was that Van should sometimes fake injuries—like, for example, by wearing unnecessary splints and bandages around me. That was for nothing, because in his few efforts at faking he always wore a look of pride.

Next, she wanted me to "compete" with Van to see if I could outdo him at having accidents. "Deprive the symptom of its message," she said, but I could never get up for that.

"I want you to notice something about yourselves," Shirley said now. This was her show of strength. She could be very seeing.

We looked ourselves over, held out our arms and hands, looked at each other.

"All right," Van said.

I said, "What?"

"You match!" Shirley said, and yes we did, in that we both had on blazers, our shirts were both made of cotton, and both of us wore jeans. My blazer was red, though, and I had on a headband. I wore sandals. My toenails were polished. Van had no purse, of course. He had socks on with his Weejuns.

"Could be coincidence?" Van asked.

"It was unplanned," I said. "We pulled on whatever we had clean."

Shirley said that from now on Van was to pick out and buy

his own clothes, and that he should start immediately, right after the session. She said he was to shop alone, and that anything he bought had to be expensive. "Buy things that *look* like you," she said.

Van wanted to know what stores.

"Let me backtrack," I said. "You say Van must do this. Why?"

I never got an answer, because Van was saying in low tones to Shirley, "I just wish it didn't have to be right now, when I'm running kind of short on money." He brought out his wallet and showed it to her. The wallet was stuffed out of shape, crammed with dollar bills. "These'd fool you," he whispered. "But they're just like receipts to me. I don't even dare think of them as money. I have to hand them straight over to the oil distributors.

Van and his uncle were co-owners of two hurting Smithco filling stations; hurting partly because we lived in an area of very low populace, in Sketching—Pennsylvania not Connecticut— and too damned far from the turnpike.

I had a little money of my own. I said, "What if I were to lend Van the dough for these new clothes?"

"Van?" Shirley said, a first—a three-way exchange.

"That'd be nice of her?" Van said.

But Shirley's look at me was a don't-you-dare.

One main thing about Van, that made people care for him so, was that he was glamorous, rock-star cute.

IT WAS AROUND EIGHT THAT NIGHT, AND I HAD cruised over to pick up Van at the better station, the one on South Holland. I was in his office there, which was just tacky windows, a plain floor, a calendar, a cash register, shelves of whatnot, a few fuming rags.

"Ready to go?" I said.

Van went no. He bought time by going out to put air into my tires. He tussled with the hose, shook the nozzle, pretended it was clogged or something. Tires didn't need air.

Too amazingly, he hit his shin on a metal tumbler on the way back and came to me limping, clenching his fists. He backed up against the counter, hiked the leg of his brand-new slacks, rubbed the red egg that was blooming.

"Now are you ready?" I said.

"No!" Van said. He stared into the garage a second. His uncle was deep inside, we could see, on a box, having a Dreamsicle from the machine.

"Could you please beat it?" Van asked me.

"Of course not, silly. How would you get home?"

"I couldn't care, it doesn't matter," Van said. "Couldn't you just leave? I was doing okay until you came."

There were no cars at the pumps, but I could tell Van wanted an excuse to get out of the office. He kept glancing back at the highway, trying to summon a customer. He looked good, as always, but he looked as if he itched.

"Let's stand back a minute," I said, karate-chopping the air. "Did Mrs. Salizar put you up to this, Van? This is the new thing, right? You're to be rude to me. Because if she did, she's going to be minus two patients. We're not shelling out the fifty-five bucks for new ways to start fights."

"I'm not fighting. But I still wish you'd go."

"We are paying to get you fixed up," I went on. "You. Because you might be in danger of really killing yourself with one of your accidents."

Van started to cry. I couldn't believe it. "You're *crying?*" I said.

I couldn't handle it at all. I asked him to stop. I said I'd yell for his uncle. Van wouldn't stop, though. He couldn't.

"I am *leaving!*" I said.

"LOOK AT THE PROCESS, NOT AT THE CONTENT," Shirley's tiny voice told me later over the telephone.

"And what does that mean?"

"That any shift in the movement is a good sign. This is excellent for Van. A sure turn for the better."

"Okay, I'm convinced. But where is he? It's midnight," I exaggerated.

I was lying in bed under the top sheet. I had been waiting and waiting.

I had left a trail of lights: a spotlight so Van could navigate from the lane, where his uncle would deposit him, to our front porch; the porch light with the yellow anti-insect bulb; a standing floor lamp on inside the foyer; the stairs lit brightly from overhead; a table lamp on in the hallway, and I had removed the manila shade; a seventy-five watter in the reading lamp just inside the bedroom. I listed these for Shirley, and said, "I'm taking no risks."

"How would you feel about going to sleep?" Shirley asked me, which was weird because she had never before asked me how I'd feel about anything.

"Forget it," I said. "Suppose something happens. I'm the only one within screaming distance. We don't have one neighbor."

"Maybe the real reason you're staying awake is that you're hurt and that's got you charged up," Shirley said. "Could that be it? The truth now, because you're sharp enough to see that whether Van comes home or doesn't, he'll be fine. He's going to be fine."

"Oh, hell," I said, realizing. "You talked to Van. You *know* he's not going to show."

"He's not going to show," the marriage counselor said.

In Jewel

I COULD BE GETTING MARRIED SOON. THE FELLOW IS no Adonis, but what do I care about that? I'd be leaving my job at the high school. I teach art. In fact, I'd be leaving Jewel if I got married.

I have six smart students, total, but only two with any talent, both in third period. One of them might make it out of here someday. I don't know. Jewel is coal mining, and it's infuriatingly true that all the kids end up in the mine.

One of my two talented students is a girl. She's involved with the mine already—works after school driving a coal truck for them. I've had her in class since her freshman year. She's got a ready mind that would have wowed them at the design school in Rhode Island where I took a degree ten or so years ago. "Dirty Thoughts," she titles all her pieces, one after another. "Here's D.T. 189," she'll say to me, holding up some contraption. She does very clever work with plaster and torn paper bags.

Jack's the name of the man I might marry. He's a sharp lawyer. He looks kind of like a poor relation, but juries feel cozy and relaxed with him. They go his way as if he were a cousin they're trying to help along.

Jack's a miner's best friend. He has a case pending now about this mammoth rock that's hanging near the top of a mountain out on the edge of town. And the mountain's on fire inside. There's a seam of coal in it that's been burning for over a year, breaking the mountain's back, and someday the rock's going to come tumbling straight down and smush the Benjamin house, it looks like, and maybe tear out part of the neighborhood.

The whole Benjamin family has seen this in their dreams.

"Hit the company now," Jack says. "Before the rock arrives."

JACK FIRST MET ME WHEN A STUDENT OF MINE WAS killed a couple years ago, and the boy's parents hired Jack to file suit against the company. As I understood it, there were these posts every few or so feet in the mine, and the company had saved a buck skipping every third post. Well, Rick, the boy—he was a senior at school but he worked afternoon half-shifts in the mine—was down in the shaft one day, and some ceiling where there wasn't a post caved in and he died on the spot. Rick was a kid who was *never* going to be a miner. His ceramics, done for me, weren't bad, when they didn't explode in the kiln.

Jack asked me out for coffee one of those days when court was in recess. We blew a couple of hours at the Ballpark Lounge playing the video game Space Invaders.

"You could win money at this," Jack said. "You ought to have your own machine."

Don't I wish. But that's how Jack thinks: big.

My gifted student who might get out of Jewel someday is

Michael Fitch. "Maybe I'm nuts," he said to me after homeroom had cleared out one morning. I have him for art and homeroom.

"I don't mind," I said.

"There's a lot of noise because I won't say the Pledge of Allegiance in assemblies," Michael said. "I refuse."

"You got to stay alert from now on, Michael," I told him. "For the next little bit, you'll have to be on your toes."

He took a pink stick of chalk to the blackboard and worked in thick, porous contours. Clouds, maybe. "I think the entire town's afraid of me," he said.

"Probably," I said.

JACK AND I WOULD GO LIVE IN CHARLESTON IF WE got married. We've talked about being there by the end of August. He even has a house lined up. Actually, it's half a house. The downstairs is a crisis center where they take "hot line" calls. Jack says I could work there if I want to work. He got me to spend an afternoon with the people, learning their procedure. They listen to these calls, I found out, and then they more or less repeat back whatever the caller's just said. Such as "You discovered your dearest friend in bed with your husband." Then they add something like "You sound angry."

Jack thinks I'd be terrific at this sort of thing. He doesn't realize my worst moments as a teacher are when somebody confides in me.

Brad Foley, for example. He confessed about some stuff he was going through with his dad, and when we were finished talking, Brad, crying, asked if he could kiss me. I said he could hug me, the poor thing, but just for a second.

I wouldn't mind waving good-bye to Jewel. But it would be tough leaving my family. Mom's all right here, and so is Russell, my big brother. Russell recently got Mom a new clothes washer. He does things like that, and they're a very contented couple.

Russell's nuts, though. I mean, here's a guy working in three feet of coal every day, contending with a couple kinds of gases that are there, also the dust from the machines, but all he wants is to be allowed to smoke cigarettes. He says it isn't because of methane that you can't smoke in the mine, it's dollars. Most of the miners roll their own cigarettes, you see, which takes a minute or two. So you figure a couple of dozen smokes would cost the company a half hour's time, every shift.

I get sad for Russell. The biggest achievement in his life is being respectable. He'd cheat and lie before he'd do anything that's frowned upon.

But I was always respectable, I admit. Two years in a row I won the Jaycees' Good Citizenship award—women's branch. Really, though, that was for my dad. I couldn't like Dad, but I often pleased him. He was superstitious about women ever working in the mines, and very confident about his opinions, which weren't backed by anything but his fears. He would hate that there are five women down there now. If he were alive, he'd be yelling about it.

The women won't last long. They'll get sick or quit for some reason. You can't blame them—it's no fun making everyone nervous.

My fiancé doesn't get too excited or too blue. He won't allow himself. He's learned to take comfort in small things. Say if he finds a word he likes, he speaks it with relish. He makes you enjoy the word with him—its aptness or strength. "I like a shower head that throws an *aggressive* spray," he says, and leans on that word "aggressive." Or he tells you that for supper he can get by gladly with a plate of fresh yellow tomatoes and just a mug of coffee, so long as the coffee is "pitchy." "Make mine tar," he says.

ONE THING THAT BOTHERS ME ABOUT LEAVING JEWEL is that I just wallpapered my bedroom at Mom's. The wallpaper I put up has a poppy pattern that's like Matisse.

Charleston wouldn't thrill Jack for long, I bet. He's headed for growth—Atlanta, Houston, D.C.

You name it and it went wrong for me up in Rhode Island. I got mangled or something. I was at the School of Design there. I finally did graduate, or some version of me graduated. I really wasn't present. I'd be walking on Thayer Street and all of a sudden realize I was looking for my reflection in every shop window.

Those who say you can't go home again haven't been to Jewel. To me, it's more like you can't *leave* home.

Back in Jewel again—surprise—I was fine.

But imagine teaching at the same high school where you and your whole family went.

It can't be good.

I figured out my dad was a freshman there in 1924.

Some days, the Rhode Island thing seems like a dream. I'll be pushing a cart around the market here, say, and it comes to me that I know all the people in the store—first and last names. I know the meat cutter. I was a Camp Fire Girl with Marsha, who works the checkout counter. I went through twelve grades with the milk guy, Lewis, who loads the dairy refrigerator. I even know what grief sends his family running to the therapist at the new guidance center. And, outside, those Leahy brothers, with their beef-red faces, on their bench on the courthouse lawn, I know, and Sue Forrest, pacing around carrying a sandwich board for her son's bakery, and the guys crowding the Ballpark Lounge and the Servo Hardware.

So, I like feeling at home. I just wish I didn't feel it here.

Little Brad Foley sent me a note of congratulations when he found out from the newspaper that Jack and I got engaged. "I hope for your sake you'll be moving," Brad wrote me.

The note's still on the shelf of my secretary.

I don't throw anything away.

No, worse—I don't *put* anything away. All that I've ever owned or had is right out here for you to look at.

The Nature of
Almost Everything

TELL YOU, AT THIRTY-SIX, MY GOALS ARE TO STAY sober and pay off my MasterCard bill. Right at the moment I'm parked in my boss's Jaguar on a road above the glen, with CBU-FM rattling bluegrass and the heater on all the way because Yellow Springs is taking a hammering this winter. I have a view of some kids doing a combination kickball and keep-away: genderless children, robotian because of their square bundling, a little spooky in the moon's skimpy light. I am having a rough time.

I try meditating, concentrate on the number one, envision a one, chant: "One, one, one, one, one, one, one, one." It doesn't help a bit. What baloney.

I'm an employee of Rad Cookerman, who owns the Cookie's Convenience Marts, and who runs for mayor every four years but never wins. Cookie just likes himself advertised. If he could get his head up on one of those lighted revolving buckets like Colonel Sanders, he probably would.

I live on Cookie's property, in a big bland house behind his small elaborate one, a couple of miles from the Antioch campus here.

I write speeches for Cookie, only he's almost never invited to speak, so the job is a real comedown from when I wrote for Senator Secrest, whom I wrote for until he died. I wrote his famous "Tonight, the lights will dim . . ." anti-execution speech, in fact.

But mostly you'd have to say mine is a cosmetic addition to the Cookerman campaign. I can look classy. For instance, I deeply admire this Chesterfield I'm wearing, and it's a good thing I stuck it on, because underneath I feel pretty defenseless. I feel stripped of about everything but the unchangeables—like height and eye color. We had a confrontation, Cookie and I, kind of severe.

He's made of money, and he pays me well, but he pays me monthly. By now, minus what I had to send the MasterCard folks—my worst charges over the years were for a brass bed frame, a harpsichord, and then, to get over my senator dying, a round-trip to Italy—I've practically finished my funds. There's no dining out for me, and the deal with dining in is that whenever I do, Cookie notices and strolls on back to my place to help me eat my food. This evening, for one, he not only appeared, glad and happy to sup, he dragged along a pal.

He had, more than once recently, insisted, "Gardenia, you're going to go gaga over my new night manager."

I'm actually called Gardenia.

Now, I saw instantly why Cookie would assume I'd be compatible with his night manager. If I had a twin, this fellow would be it. Nordic; same crooked nose, and big-boned like me; blond hair probably even cropped by Freddy at Hairsnips. I can't figure why people want to put you together with an opposite-sex version of yourself, but experience says they do.

Cookie, through the entire first half hour of supper, held forth on the hero of his youth, Rod Serling. I should get three college credits for the times I've listened uncritically to Cookie tell about Mr. Serling's days at Antioch. And Cookie's voice is a trial—way down there in Waylon Jennings land, and slow! His sentences take forever.

This Jag seat has the odor of newness and Cookie's first-choice scent, Bay Rum.

So, eventually, Cookie must've deduced I wasn't leveled by his night manager, who, if he possessed the gift of speech, kept it secret. Night manager would point north up the table, say, so that I'd pass him the three possibles before he'd indicate—nod—he had meant the sesame breadsticks.

Jesus.

I'm leaning hard into the car door here. The heater's making contact with only my lower parts. My feet and calves are roasted, the rest of me's chilled to pain. This sad feeling that's got me has a manic ass-ugly flip side, I know, and there's an icy little limbo you get to go through in between.

Cookie loaded up on me, really. He put me against the ropes. He started by making insinuations about the chicken cacciatore—asking did I get the recipe from the back of a ketchup bottle and exactly how many bottles of ketchup had they told me to use? I can't say I wasn't injured. And he made worse remarks, and there began to be, behind his half smile, a look of strain, as if he didn't want to crush me, but if he had to, he had to. Cookie has a wandering left eyeball, and ordinarily I forget about it. But during his barrage, the eyeball went rolling wild. So much worminess could not be healthy for Cookie, but that is his hard luck. Mine's how extremely much I would like a margarita, please, or a hot buttered rum. I still have a tomato-y, yes, ketchupy, taste on my tongue, goddamn it.

I'M OUT OF THE CAR NOW AND DOWN THE STEPS into the glen, though it's that stark-still kind of cold, and pitch dark. Did I tell you there've been murders committed here?

I've caused a sputtering of birds—just birds. I find a lacquered bench that's so frosted over, my rump goes right-away numb.

So quiet.

I'm clenching myself and I'm, in my fashion, praying, because a drinking binge would be a very negative way for me to go, next.

It's weird. I'm a complete atheist, but I get a whoosh feeling and something flies off my chest.

I'm all right, now.

I wouldn't take a drink if you forced me.

Back to the Jag, only this time, no radio. I've got to perfect an apology to Cookie for swiping his car. I'll summon my speech-writing powers. I'll even enjoy it. The thing is, you take away the call of the cocktail, and I'm happy as a clam.

Nothing's It

RIDING ON THE BACK BED OF THE TRUCK, HIGH ON top of the sacks of mulch, is Devon, wondering where to look. He has already exchanged smiles with the freckle-faced girl in the car following.

Foss is below, driving in a cabin filled with boxes. Foss owns the nursery where Devon is a laborer. The truck's headed cross-city, to Foss's home and, on the way, to Devon's Newbury Street apartment.

Winter's giving Boston a good one. Devon's face is red, hardened from the cold. He gazes leftward at an impoverished lot of used motorcycles. There are two Suzukis and a worn Bonneville there that Devon regards with a longing growl. He switches his face at some passing brownstones, makes up an expression, and nods at a second-story window that has a Virgin Mother statue on the sill. A horn pips. The freckle-faced girl waves farewell as her Datsun veers into the turnoff lane. Devon grins helplessly, feeling dumb. Another car with another girl moves into position behind the nursery truck. Devon opens his hand on his thigh and stares at the fingers, studying nothing.

They reach Back Bay. Foss puts half the truck on the runner of sidewalk in front of Devon's building and bumps to a stop. "All right!" he yells back as Devon drops easily down. "See you bright and early! Too damned early!"

"Got you!" Devon says, and the truck guns off.

Devon likes Foss, but supposes he shouldn't. They are roughly the same age—both into their thirties—and Foss owns the business where Devon is only a worker. Today, they worked Haymarket Cemetery. Foss ran a backhoe while Devon shoveled and then raked litter.

Inside the granite building where he has now lived a month, Devon checks the mail, takes the steps on the fly, feeds his key into the apartment's lock.

"It's me, sorely cold," he says to the front room. He closes the door behind him with a slamming kick, not because he is angry, but so Nobuko will know he's home.

From the bedroom comes the monotonous putter of the movie projector.

Nobuko is on the bed, in her blue silk pajamas. Behind her, on a bureau, a Super-8 machine is running through a reel, spraying light. Nobuko, lying flat, has a square of laundry cardboard which she holds up into the fan of illumination. She catches a piece of face, a tangle of moving shrubs, part of a car in bright color on the card. They flicker away. She tilts the card and a laughing face distorts—stretching horizontally. She runs the image farther left, until the eyes and mouth tear, then lets the picture spill off entirely.

"It's me," Devon says.

"Hello," Nobuko says, and sighs.

THE MOVIES ARE FROM DEVON'S FAMILY. NOBUKO has spliced and cemented together ten or twelve reels—a Wyoming trip, Devon's B.U. graduation, Devon's grandfather's retirement house, Devon lifting weights in a garage.

"I'm aching with cold," he says.

He stands beside Nobuko. On the card now is a bit of sky from a movie of Devon's new dog, made by Devon's older brother when Devon was thirteen. Nobuko shakes her arm and the blue clouds undulate like water.

"If you move that thing down some, you'll catch me and my hound," Devon says. "Buster."

Nobuko sits up, reaches behind, and twists a knob, killing the projector.

"You have some of the nicest clothes," Devon says, "but I never see them. I mean, you only wear those p.j.'s."

Nobuko puts herself on her stomach, and folds part of her pillow against her black hair.

"Nothing to eat?" Devon says. "Tell me what's the matter."

"What's the matter?" he would say in the mornings before he left for work, and in the evenings when he returned.

"There are things," Nobuko says. "Many things."

"Lassitude?" Devon says. "Or is it depression?"

"I may leave," she says.

THEY'D MET IN A BAR, A CHOWDER AND BEER PLACE, off Beacon Street, called The Ships. Nobuko was helping the bartender trim a tabletop Christmas tree, hanging her origami work among the bulbs. Devon, drinking up some holiday gift money, watched from down the counter as Nobuko deftly fanned and folded. She made clusters of tiny flowers. She made birds in flight, and angel dolls.

"Anything," he said, when Nobuko caught him staring. "Anything at all I can do for you."

"That's nice of you," she said.

"I live upstairs," Devon said, and that night Nobuko went to see his rooms, and stayed.

But after a week, she lived less in the apartment over The Ships than in the bar below and on the street out front. She had a peddler's license, and she set up a stand there and sold the things she made. She wore layers of heavy clothing, and went in and out of the bar all day. She knew dozens of people—she talked with everybody.

Devon found work at the nursery and moved them, the next autumn, to the Back Bay place, which was bigger, lighter, safer. They took the apartment over on a World Series Saturday, and as Devon carried in labeled boxes and his old furniture, he wore a transistor radio on a wrist strap, for the game.

Nobuko set up the three-piece stereo, donned her blue silk pajamas, and parked their deepest armchair by a loudspeaker.

She went under headphones, shutting out Devon and closing her eyes.

The next day, Devon laundered his shirts in the basement machines. He spray-starched and ironed them. He hung them in a bedroom closet, arranging them by hue—darkest to lightest. With a bristly brush he scrubbed the thick canvas coveralls that were his work suits.

Nobuko used the earphones, or ran her movie projector, or folded paper.

By evening, Devon had lettered his name and Nobuko's on the framed card on their front door. He had hammered all the necessary brackets for curtain rods. He had put together their bed.

But after that Sunday, the rest of their belongings stayed in boxes. Weeks went, and nothing got put away. When Devon needed a spoon, or a drinking glass, or playing cards, or kitchen shears, he had to hunt through the crates.

"HELP ME OUT," DEVON SAYS NOW. "JUST LOOK at me."

Nobuko turns slowly in the sheets and blankets. She tries a smile, but it fades quickly. "You look done in," she tells him.

"I'm killing myself," he says. "I'm not used to having a job this hard, and doing it this faithfully. You know what I mean?"

"Maybe. No," she says.

In the kitchen, he opens and heats two cans of chili. He warms a healthy splash of rum in a saucepan and swallows the drink for its fire. He thinks of Nobuko's parents in San Jose.

He hurries back to the bedroom. "Could your parents be of any help to you?"

"I can get by," Nobuko says. She shrugs. "They don't want to know about it."

For the hundredth time, Devon asks Nobuko to marry him.

"Oh, no, Devon. Un unh," she says.

"We'll do better than this. We can do better than this place here. And my job, I mean. If that's it."

"Nothing's it," Nobuko says.

"GIVE HER MY BEST. TELL HER TO BUCK UP. TELL HER Johnny Foss wants her to get better," Foss says.

"That'll help," Devon says.

"In two more seconds," Foss says, "I'm going right over the top of that pea-brain in the Fiat."

"I can walk from here," Devon says. He hops from the cabin of the Foss Nursery truck, which has been stalled in a Friday-night traffic tangle.

"Hey, Devon! Give her my best," Foss says. "It's tough."

"Take it easy for the weekend," Devon says.

He starts jogging. There are chains of Christmas lights across the streets. A drugstore window is full of gold-foil candy boxes belted with fancy ribbons. A lot of car horns are ringing.

Devon checks the mailbox, finds a gas bill and a newspaper page from a hardware store. He takes the steps, opens the door.

Nobuko is sitting with someone. Her headphones are off, resting on the back of her neck. On a packing crate between her and the stranger is an assortment of plastic items—a shoehorn, key chains, a ruler, a medicine spoon. All the items are printed with the names, addresses, and slogans of local merchants.

"Hi," Devon says.

"Hello Neighbor Club," the stranger says.

"Neighbor Club," Nobuko says.

The visitor is a man about forty. He's dimpled, with a happy, careless-looking face, and a sloppy necktie. He shows Devon his dimples, and picks up his spiel. "Rush is a client I really feel good about backing. In fact, really all our clients are good people and they provide excellent service, but especially Rush."

Devon takes a seat on the floor by the packing crate. He examines the shoehorn. He reads, "Pulaski's—Where The Shoe Fits." The key chain, he notices, is from Foss's Nursery and Gardening Center.

"We don't go to stores," Nobuko says.

"You never go, eh?" the man says, brightly. "Well, you may need to someday, when one of our little future Red Sox down on the street hits a home run through your window. That's when you may want to think about window glass. And to get you thinking about the right people for glass, Donnelly's would like me to give you this cap gripper. It's a thing you'll use ten times a day, if you're like me. Loosens jar lids and does twist-off caps that won't twist. I'm Burt Libby."

"Devon," Devon says. "I like those gripper things."

"Well, this one's yours. And another advantage of Donnelly's is they have a frame-it-yourself department, which you can walk out of after an hour with your picture or art work perfectly framed under glass and ready to hang. Unless you're like my wife and putter over which mat goes with which molding."

"We aren't like her. We wouldn't go there," Nobuko says.

"Oh, now, we might," Devon says, laughing. "You never know. So, what's the rest of this stuff? We get to keep it?"

"Sure. See, it cooks down to this. The businessman wants to get you into his store one time, whether you'll buy or not. That way, you know what he's got and how to find him. So, plus what you see here, if you visit any of the places on the list I give you, they each have an additional goody for you when you go in."

"We don't need any of it," Nobuko says.

"That's fine and dandy. I'm not here to sell you a thing."

Devon reaches for Nobuko's foot, which is near him—a foot that hasn't worn shoes in weeks.

The man says, "I think I may have interrupted your wife's musical concert. You two knew I was coming?"

"Yeah. I remember you called," Devon says. "*We* set it up, in fact, I think."

"I could come back, when your wife's feeling better."

"We're all right," Devon says.

Nobuko is absentmindedly fingering a paper coupon the man has given her. With one hand she folds and unfolds, eventually producing a little animal with an oversized head.

"Let me get you coffee or something," Devon says to the man. "Out here in the kitchen."

On the wall next to the stove, Devon has tacked up a hoop of pine branches got at discount from Foss's, and some of Nobuko's origami doodles.

"Her work," Devon says.

"Yes."

"You've seen the living room. Around there's the bathroom."

"A big kitchen," the man says.

"You should've seen what we had before," Devon says.

"Bedroom through there?" asks the man.

"You can look at it if you want while I get this coffee put together, or I think we have cider."

"No, we don't!" Nobuko calls out.

"How long have you been here?" the man says.

"We just got in, really. I mean, it's still in the planning stages." Devon gets a flame moving under a kettle, and then he leads the man into the bedroom. "Just my shirts," he says, swinging the closet door.

"Movies?" the man says.

"Yeah, the projector," Devon says.

"You make movies, or just watch them?"

"Just watch them. They're just some home movies," Devon says.

"So you get some popcorn and candy and get into bed. Very cozy."

"They are *my* movies!" Nobuko yells. The Hello Neighbor man raises his eyebrows and smirks. "What, exactly, is wrong with that woman?"

Devon pushes the man, using the heels of both hands. The Foss Nursery job has made Devon strong, so the shove sends the man backward.

"Out," Devon says.

The man stands cautiously and edges around Devon.

"This is one I'll remember," he says.

DEVON IS UP LATE FOR A WEEKNIGHT. BESIDE HIM on the thrift-shop couch, Nobuko is curled into a ball. She is falling asleep with her cheek on Devon's thigh.

"So nice," he says.

"You've been saying that a lot."

"You've been letting me say it," he says.

Nobuko says, "You remember Patsy DeSoto?"

"With the violin? And the parakeet? A beggar?"

"From Beacon Street, yeah," Nobuko says. "I really miss seeing her. I miss her music. I miss being out there, seeing everybody. There's so much that's happening on the street. Everybody knows me. You know, here comes Ted Kennedy or a parade of Italian guys. Lots of people say, 'There's Nobuko,' like they're so glad to see me. Accidents happen. I got a lot of friends there. Reporters. That sidewalk artist? You bought him chalk once. Mike something?"

"Yeah, I did," Devon says. "But I always thought Mike was just losing time. He did some nice stuff, but it all got walked on and rained on and the dogs, of course."

"Being out there. Seeing everybody," Nobuko says. "*That's* the story."

Look at Me Go

THERE WAS A FAINT, INDUSTRIAL HUM I THOUGHT I heard, and from up the beach the sound of swings creaking on chains, and a grinding noise from the spinning playground machine I've always called a whiz-around.

There *was* a lighthouse, but it seemed ineffectual—like an amusement park thing. The day was pale. White glinted off the water. The sun was white. There was a breeze with autumn in it. The swimming season was almost over.

At the next bench in the long shelter, a bare-chested man with a cord for a belt was lecturing quietly to his boy in Russian. Over that, Paul had the portable radio going, and we sat regarding the water, Paul and I.

A collection of college kids in Yale sweat shirts were ruining their jogging shoes in the cold tide. There was a lifeguard with a whistle clamped in his teeth. He had found a length of crooked stick and was playing fetch with a wet spaniel.

A little storm arrived. The lifeguard sent his dog walking and towed a safety boat closer to his stand. He went out onto a rock jetty to watch the sky. A jagged pin of lightning blinked, but far across the sound.

Two boys younger than Paul—twelve, maybe—took over the guard's tower. Down from the tower on a red towel, a woman in a fading suit shifted carelessly in her sleep and let her knees fall open. The pushing wind mixed up brown sand and shell splinters. A cat-food ad crackled from Paul's radio.

The Point had been a purposeless stop on a restless Saturday drive I was doing with my son. We had followed signs.

Before that, I had had a bad fight with my husband, Jeff. Jeff was using the telephone at the time. He was on "hold."

"I don't trust Paulie," Jeff said to me, his fingers guarding the telephone's mouthpiece. "I mean, I love him, he's my son. I almost never believe him, though, and I'm sure he lies. I think he's a fraud."

I remember reeling into the bedroom to get my set of car keys. I spent some time in there, angrily stroking my hair. I buttoned some clothes on—a cardigan. I didn't bother with makeup, or even tying my tennis shoes.

Jeff was still on the phone as I came back through the library. "Look, it's not just you," he was saying. "We're all waiting on the shipment." Jeff was executive salesman for a furniture store.

I let the dog in off the balcony where she'd been barking away.

"I've taken orders, too, Johnny," Jeff said to the phone. "I could use the commissions, too. You want their home office number? I mean, you're more than welcome to get them and try to shake them up. More than welcome."

I went back out onto the balcony. "Paulie!" I yelled to the

yard, to the neighborhood in general. Paul was out there somewhere. He hadn't heard what his father had said. Paul was four-
teen; our only child.

Inside again, I teased around with the dog, tussling with her
over a rubber bone that had a jingle bell. I was waiting for Jeff.

"Hold it one minute," he said to me, and then to the phone,
"Maybe you ought to pay attention more, friend." He listened,
and said, "I just don't believe that."

FOR ALL THE SKYWORKS, THERE REALLY WASN'T
much rain.

Paul had got off our bench and moved around the Russian
boy. The boy had a horseshoe crab in his capture. "Badness!"
Paul said. He did his girlish giggle.

"It's like a helmet, don't you think?" asked the Russian boy.
He tipped over the crab and revealed its jointed, struggling
limbs. Paul yelped, bopped the boy on the shoulder, ran away,
and came back again.

The Russian father strolled over to my bench. His bare
shoulders had been dampened by the meager rain. He had the
big girth and rolling muscles of a laborer.

A voice on Paul's radio talked about Coleman Coolers. Our
boys knelt together, drizzling sand onto the crab.

"This one sleeps hard," the Russian man said, smiling off at
the woman on the red towel. She was in a sprawl.

Thunder murmured. The lifeguard's whistle chirped in
a three-beat pattern. The woman drew herself up, curved her
spine, stretching. She headed for the shelter.

"Your sister?" the Russian man asked me.

The Yale students—five of them—aimed their running game of plastic football for the shelter, although they were already soaked. The one girl in the pack collapsed onto a bench just down from mine. A young man with white ointment on his nose charged up and put himself on her lap. "Oof," the Yale girl said.

Her young man said something like, "Das vi danya," to the Russian, and, "Stras vu eatya."

"Thank you," the Russian said.

My Paul tugged at his cotton-lisle shirt, fought his way out of it, and spread it on the sand. The other boy lowered the crab onto the shirt. The two began dragging the crab around, giving it a ride. They left a little wake on the rain-speckled beach.

Paul's chest looked dough-white, and his arms tubular next to the toned body of the Russian boy.

The university students must have thought I was married to the Russian father. They spoke to us as a couple. They asked us about the Soviet Union.

"What do I know?" the Russian said. "That was such a long time past."

"We're in for it, weatherwise," said the young fellow with the nose ointment. "Big storm due."

"They called that off," his girl friend said. "Come on, Dan. Will you get up? My legs are getting numb."

Paul skipped up to me. "You should see its eyes," he said.

"Paulie, stop wiggling," I said. "Get your shirt back on."

"Watch," he said. He spun and did a gawky sprint for the water. He was proud of his imagined speed. He often referred to it. *Look at me go.* Things like that.

"Some kids get big real fast," said the Russian father. "Some other kids get to be kids a long time. I think they're more lucky."

His boy called out to Paul, "What's your time in the hundred?"

Paul was by the water, out of breath, bent at the waist, his hands on his knees. "Ten-five," he managed.

"I'm sure," the Yale girl said.

"I sort of doubt it," her friend, Dan, said.

"No, I think that's right," I said. "My husband timed him with a stopwatch."

"Better fix his stopwatch," Dan said.

"It could be," the Russian father said. He smiled as though he loved all boys and took pride in them—even mine. He smiled as though he loved *me*. I let it come, so much love so easy.

© Pier Rodelon

MARY ROBISON was born in Washington, D.C. She is the recipient of a Guggenheim Fellowship, two Pushcart Prizes, an O. Henry Award, the Los Angeles Times Book Prize for Fiction, and the 2018 Arts and Letters Award in Literature. She is the author of four novels and four story collections. She lives in Gainesville, Florida.

Printed in the United States
by Baker & Taylor Publisher Services